soulnotskin

ISBN 978-1-7339508-1-7 (Paperback Edition)

Author photo: Glenn Silva Photography
Writing coach: Chocoloate Readings
Editor: Author Connections, LLC

Printed in the United States of America

www.soulnotskin.com

soulnotskin

*becoming the me I was
meant to be*

JEN SLUMAC

This book is dedicated to all of us.
Let's keep growing
in faith and hope and humanity.
We're in this together.

INTRODUCTION

When we are children, impactful moments freeze, like a Polaroid that will be carried into adulthood. Each shot is proof of a time that frightened or excited us, placing itself before all other events as they occur. The mundane, mildly pleasing, gentle moments— those are all lost to the prominence of bolder snapshots.

The inherent temperament of a child acts as a filter to their lens. Morbidly treasured moments are incessantly reviewed and discussed as if displayed in a gallery of personal, precious pain, evidence of being different from the rest. This is the ticket that explains the loneliness, it fortifies the *us* and *them*. The human being wants to be distinguished. Unique.

A collection of fragmented memories and childhood souvenirs, patched together, create the narrative of an individual's life; the shoddy quilt often anemic in its representation of the whole. Other actors captured are caught off guard, like strangers in the background of vacation photos. They are merely passing by, living their own lives. They are also busy growing up. They are busy in the process of dismantling their own narrative's hold on them.

And we collide.

We are all captured in the Polaroids of others, though we may never know whose.

Compassion and forgiveness are essential to moving forward in a healthy state.

Collisions are, after all, usually accidents.

CHAPTER ONE

My poor mother wrestled me, kicking and screaming, into lace dresses and buckle-shoes every Sunday morning. I was a fraud in pigtails—a liar to all who adored and praised me while I kicked to resist suffocating the tomboy in me. I asked Mom why she made me wear those girlie things, even though I knew what she would say. "We're going to God's house and we dress nicely to show Him respect."

I was raised in a world that misunderstood my closest friend, whom they called God. I don't recall a distinct introduction to the God idea, but I was born seeking kinship beyond my lineage. I perceived more than myself in this world long before I would witness it. Cries from the hungry, the oppressed, and the poor. The weight of an addict's desperation and the silent sadness of those forgotten—these things congested the highway of my empathic nervous system from a relatively early age. I'd bite the insides of my cheeks to anchor myself—always bracing my young body, lest people see the inner commotion. I walked gingerly at times for fear of energy overflow.

I saw how people can misrepresent God with the best of intentions. What I experienced inside was invisible to others, even as it consumed me. I'd attempt to articulate it and be told either that I was smart or that I think too much. People were either intrigued or bored and would disengage. I decided that to fit in, I needed to talk less, stifle my voice, silence my thoughts.

The knowledge of something bigger than myself goes back to my earliest days, as far as I can remember. A sense of something more was always with me, and I would spend a lifetime learning to process that understanding; eventually writing this book. Ultimately, it was the God idea that I allowed to organize me. I knew God was pure love and His investment was in hearts and minds—neither of which had anything to do with the fanciness of shoes on my feet. At five years old I already sensed that something was wrong.

I learned to use the word God in church, at dinner when we said grace, and at bedtime when we said prayers. God was a word we used like 'hello' or 'goodbye.' It may as well have been a word like 'door' or 'spaghetti'. I learned that God is a He and people always pointed to the sky when they referred to Him. I learned plenty of things about a male God, most of which didn't make sense to me.

I began keeping secrets as a young girl, because I couldn't help observing the discrepancies between what people claimed to value and how they behaved. I was taught things I was expected to believe, but I wasn't emotionally connected to the idea of God that others believed. I grew discouraged. People described Him as angry, with lots of rules, and I heard that He liked some people while He hated others. People told me that God hated gay people. Eventually, that meant me. None of this fit my idea of God. I grew shameful.

On the contrary, my friend God knew everything I thought about, so it didn't occur to me that I was different. Long before I developed in my sexuality, I kept secrets to avoid carrying the confusion I saw in other people, but God and I were good.

My experience was that although God was invisible, He gave me a feeling of security. I was comfortable in my own skin with this friend known as God. I couldn't see it, understand it, or describe it, but His presence made me happy. It was a knowing, and when I thought about it, I felt accepted, welcome, and enveloped by love.

The concrete driveway was wide enough for me to stumble several times and still not reach the lawn. I wouldn't get yelled at if I was on the lawn; that was my landing pad. I saved the grass for the end. My arms stretched as far as possible so I could feel closer to the world as I spun. I closed my eyes, wanting to reach far enough into the invisible that I might touch something real and true. That's how tight I closed my eyes, how far I reached, how fast I spun.

My breathing was heavy from excitement and constant circle spins. I had been telling myself, just one more, for two minutes. Eventually my circles got sloppy and I stumbled, panting and sweating, toppling to the green earth and rolling onto my back. I loved being out of breath and dizzy, watching the clouds swirl above me. All was blurry and I could not catch my breath, which made me giggle.

To any watching eyes I was alone on the lawn, but I was actually playing with God, who I just knew was with me beyond the clouds. I expected that He was dizzy, too. We played together. The distorted perception and heavy breathing and endorphins surging were his gifts to me. With Him I was able to step outside of the real world. I'd ask Him what to do when I was confused. I could tell Him when I was happy or scared. He was my best friend. We belonged to each other.

* * *

When I was a little girl, church was a safe place. We lived next door in the manse— the house where a Presbyterian minister and his family live as part of his salary. The property around the church and the manse was our playground. I grew up digging in the dirt behind bushes, climbing fire escapes, and hiding on roofs, playing basketball in the driveway with my brother and kids from the neighborhood. Mom and Dad spent all of their time between the two buildings, so both felt like they were part of my home. We moved between the two buildings like they were rooms in a single house. "I'm going to my office" was just another room in the house, even though Dad had to walk outside and go to the church to get there. Mom went to choir practice and cooked for church events in the big kitchen. Dad was there, too; meeting with people from the congregation, writing his sermons, and practicing choir. Our church did variety shows and they were a lot of fun. There was singing, laughter, food, and fellowship.

My mom was young and beautiful. From the front pews where I always found a seat, I could see her clearly in the choir. She stood out among the others, because, while they were all costumed in the same choir robes, she was younger than most at about thirty-five years old. She had a soft brown Dutch-boy haircut that framed her blue eyes and smile. I liked watching her put make-up on in the bathroom. My witness stand was the toilet. I would pull my knees up close to my chin and hug them, watching every detail of her transformation in a fully-captivated, slight rocking motion. Side to side I'd shift, taking mental notes for later years. Her mouth opened wide to help the mascara stick to her lashes. After brushing both top rows sideways and from the eyelid out toward the mirror, she would keep her face close to the lit glass and blink a few times. Then she would take the wand and tickle the bottom set of lashes on each eye with its tip. Body frozen, only her eyeballs would move to look at each eye with the other. Once satisfied, she'd look at me and ask, "how's that?" and close the mascara.

The familiar noises that accompanied her regimen; the in and out pump of the wand into the tube to get bristles loaded, the smacking of lips after gloss was applied, the blowing of brushes prior to application of blush or eye shadow. I can still see and hear all of it. This routine is one of those mental movies I captured in my young mind that define a time where she seemed happy, strong, and beautiful.

I have found comfort in the sounds of make-up bags and application rituals throughout my adult life. It's a precious token of a little girl watching her mother, downloading how to be a lady, a woman, a wife, and a mom.

Seeing her in the choir, we'd already shared her routine that morning and I felt close within the embrace of my parents, even though they were both up on stage. I shared them with everyone in the big, stained-glass, Christ-adorned sanctuary, but they were mine. They loved me, God loved me. I was happy.

When I was a kid living in this close circle of safety, I didn't wonder or care about what anyone thought of me; not the way I would learn to care. Long before I could read the hymnals myself, I memorized passages. Everyone else was standing, so I stood too, arms at my sides, back straight, voice facing toward the heavens, eager to please God as I recited the strange words. "Our Father who aren't in heaven, Hell would be thy name..."

As hard as I tried to be good, some things we had to say made me want to laugh; they didn't feel right. I remember being confused about language we used when we sang or prayed in church. If I laughed out loud, Mom would 'shh' me from the choir and I'd get in trouble after the service. I'd look over at my father, seated in his black robe with his fancy minister scarf around his neck. He'd have his legs crossed and his hands resting on his knee. His attentive head faced down, listening, and waiting for his turn to speak. He seemed unaware of me; we children were Mom's job. He stayed focused on being the minister. Soon he would speak from the podium. I thought it was actually his podium, and it was nice that he shared.

Every Sunday before Dad gave his sermon, other people would read something. We'd sing songs that I didn't like, and my friend and I drew pictures in our bulletins. Once she drew a hangman with X's for eyes and a tongue sticking out. She was not a great artist. I wanted to laugh but knew better, so I squeezed my whole face closed and tucked it into my chest to keep noise from bursting out of me. The tension created by pressured silence became the primary cause of a giggle-fit that earned Mom's 'look'. What was it about tension that always brought me to laughter?

The choir finished singing, and Dad called the kids up for Children's talk, which I both loved and hated. I loved Children's talk because I got to sit by my dad on the front steps of the church. Even though all the kids did this, everyone knew that the minister was my father. That made me feel important. Dad told stories about characters in the Bible, the book about God and Jesus, and then he'd ask questions. I wanted to answer, but he didn't always call on me when I raised my hand. Sometimes that hurt my feelings. He said that when Jesus was alive, he would tell stories to the children just like that, except the steps they sat on were outside. I figured my dad was like Jesus.

I hated Children's talk time because right after we finished, I had to go off to Sunday school and listen to confusing stories from people who wore smiles on their faces but seemed to be sad inside. I didn't have proof, but I felt anxiety in them while few others seemed to. I earned a reputation in some circles of being a pretty serious kid. I'd grow despondent because I wanted to be in the other room, where I wasn't allowed. Occasionally, when Sunday school was cancelled, I got to stay near the adults. I preferred being around grownups to a bunch kids who either blindly believed or easily dismissed everything we were taught. While I felt a need to consider the lessons placed before me, deciphering my own thoughts in context of my own bond with God, no other kids seemed to share my deliberate reflection in a quest for awareness.

Maybe I liked being around older people because I felt like they must know something I didn't know. Children had questions; adults had answers. I wanted answers. I wanted to stay and listen to Dad's sermon. He would be gone to his office most of the week working on it. I wanted to stay and hear what he'd written.

Since we lived right next door and I missed him, sometimes my friends and I would sneak into the church. Dad would be alone, typing in his office, and I would have races beneath the pews. Starting in the rear of the church, we'd lie on our backs and monkey-bar-propel ourselves over the waxed wooden floors. We grabbed one pew at a time and pulled ourselves into an accelerated slide to the other end. Sometimes I won, sometimes I lost. Other times I'd bang my head on the foot of a pew in an excited frenzy to beat my friends. That hurt.

When none of my friends could play, I'd go into the church alone. I took comfort sneaking into his office and hiding at the bottom of his desk. I loved the rhythmic lullaby of his typewriter keys. Every letter he struck was a note of the music he would play when he told his story on Sunday.

When Sunday mornings came and Dad performed his sermons, I would close my eyes to remember the song of his keystrokes behind the words. I wondered which parts of the story had sounded the prettiest as he typed. Dad's sermons often began with stories about my brothers and me and the things we had done that week, but every story always ended up talking about Jesus. The congregation was pin-drop-silent while he told his colorful and inspiring tales. I aspired to be like my father that way.

* * *

There was another church service about an hour after we were done. I'd sit on the lawn and watch them go inside. Every member was black, and they were always dressed up and organized in family groups. Their energy was bigger than the people in my church. They were louder as they milled about. Something about them felt familiar. Sometimes I wished I belonged to them. I wished I could slip into the crowd and get lost in it, and no one would know that I didn't belong.

But again, I would stand out. I couldn't get lost in their congregation with my blonde hair and blue eyes. I imagined I would be told to leave, that I didn't belong there either. I'd stay on the porch or the lawn and pretend to be playing, wishing someone might notice how much I wanted them to call me over and pick me up, swing me around, and call me their own. I wanted to move freely like they did. I wanted to be loud and beautiful too.

As a little girl, I wanted to understand why something in their gathering yanked at me inside. Something in the energy among their congregation tugged, trying to draw me out. I wanted to run and play and sing, but I sat still and quiet instead. Once they were all inside, I would look around to be sure no one was watching. It was then that I found a spot behind the bushes, along the outside wall of the church. I would hear the minister's voice, but not his words. I didn't need his words; I'd close my eyes and feel him. The sing-song of the sounds inside that building held me somehow. They understood that I felt different. They eased my loneliness.

In our church I was always expected to sit still and be quiet. I loved how the sounds and energy of their services ebbed and flowed. There were no walls to block the spirit that felt called to speak; there was no shame in a body that wanted to dance, a heart that wanted to cry, or lungs that needed to scream. I was in awe of their freedom and abandon in celebrating their faith. I couldn't see inside, but I would close my eyes to feel the magic. I'd hear "Amen", "Yes, Lord", "Tell It", "Make it

Plain", and "Hallelujah!" shouted out, spontaneous eruptions from the people. I wished I could see inside that church with my eyes, but I was fixed with my heart—always my clearest vision. It felt like they didn't have any secrets. It felt like they knew the pain of my heart. Their service embraced me. And then they sang. I dissolved into tears and by the end of church something felt repaired inside. I felt strong enough to pretend until next week.

When they were winding down, I had to move out of the bushes, wipe my face clean, and return to the yard. I'd act like I had been busy playing and minding my business. I'd watch the parade of beautiful people laughing, hugging, and chasing children who refused to stay in tow. I hoped one of them would see me and come over to where I sat, grab my hand, and tell me that they could see my heart. It seemed to me that even though our outsides didn't match, the people from that other congregation sang my soul and knew my heart. It felt like those strangers loved me.

I sat in my pretending because I matched the wrong side of history and I was sorry. I had already learned to not say everything I wanted to say, so I quietly prayed "I love you's" at them all and nearly brought myself to tears, ignoring what pulled at me from deep within because I didn't know how to follow it without causing a stir.

Inevitably, someone would meet my shy eyes and smile. I would breathe a deep sigh. In that moment we connected, and I belonged. In that moment, with no words exchanged, a divine kinship was exalted. In spite of all the mess that words and ideas and people create, I felt seen in a way that mattered. I felt like those eyes genuinely saw me and knew the truth. One smile and I felt real.

CHAPTER TWO

When the safe places in my life became suspect and telling the truth became a riddle, bigger secrets developed. Things that happened at home were not to be talked about outside of home. I don't know that there was ever a formal sit-down to explain these things, but I could feel the rules increasing and safety seemed dependent on figuring them out.

When I couldn't become any smaller in a corner of my flowered-wallpaper bedroom, at seven years old I decided that I had no choice. I had to tug open the sliding door and reveal the source of breaking dishes and whispered apologies. Mommy was in the chair, telling me through tears and snotty gasps that everything was fine and to go back to bed, but my father grabbed me by the shoulder, and we left the house. I was in my pajamas. We got in the blue car and went backwards, fast, out of the driveway. I remember my view from below the dashboard. The window was dark blue with blurry lights as we drove. Inside and outside it felt cold.

Suddenly the car stopped. Dad told me to lock my door and he'd be right back. I watched him disappear from my side and into the corner store. My eyes never left the door that swallowed him. Within moments he emerged holding a fountain drink and he threw away a small paper bag. I was excited he got us a Pepsi and asked for a sip. He said nothing, holding his drink away from me. He took a long pull on his red straw, exhaled loudly, and started the car. His breath was warm and sour when he leaned over to kiss my forehead, and then shook his head. I sat quietly beside him, grateful for time with him, but confused because I felt scared.

When we finally pulled into the driveway again, the blue car hit our basketball post and jolted me from my seat. I looked up at Dad to find his face squished up as he put the car in reverse and backed up a little. We were finally stopped, and he took a deep breath. We both stared straight ahead and sat in silence for a minute. He opened his door. He put one leg out to the concrete before he turned back to look at me, patted my hand, and simply said, "Home." I watched him close the door and his body disappeared from his driver window, toward the back of the car. I sat there in the quiet darkness of night as the car made clicking noises before it fell asleep.

I wished I was allowed to tell Dad that I could feel his broken heart. I wished I could kiss his face with my arms wrapped tight around his neck, but he looked so sad and angry. I wished I could sit in the car for the rest of my life because his hand touched my hand. I believe he told me he loved me through that touch. The passenger car door opened, and my mother reached in to retrieve me.

"Are you okay, honey? Let's go inside and get you to bed. Are you okay?"

"I'm tired," is all I said.

I wished I could tell her that I felt both of their broken hearts. I wished I could tell her that everyone and everything felt sad. My left hand grabbed hers, and my right thumb found its way into my mouth to keep the truth from coming out.

She tucked me in with a smile and told me she loved me, and Daddy loved me, and she sang to me like she always did. We said our prayers and asked God to take care of us. I felt nervous inside, but we behaved like everything was okay. I went to sleep.

* * *

When my parents divorced, they split friends. I learned that friends can divorce, too. It seemed like all of their friends still loved me, they just didn't love my mom anymore. I didn't know who I could talk to without upsetting things, so I became progressively quieter and existed more inside than out. In the divvying up of friendships and belongings, I believed that God had gone with Dad. When I mentioned the friends who 'went with Dad' it hurt Mom's feelings, but I looked around and didn't recognize anything or anyone anymore. I always felt anxious and unsure, and I was angry with my parents.

As security and structure dissolved at home, school became my safe place. I was at school when my principal pulled me out of class to go downtown and talk to a man about my family. He was called a counselor. Mom and Dad told me they were getting a divorce, which meant they still loved me and my brothers, but didn't love each other anymore. I would get to visit with them both. The whole time it seemed I was being told or talked at. Everything sounded like Charlie Brown's aunt. Then, suddenly, it was my turn.

The counselor smiled and leaned in toward small me in a big chair. Someone asked, "Is that okay, Jenny?" It didn't feel like a real question, so I didn't answer. I stared out the giant glass window behind the man who said my family was ending. I saw an airplane and people working on a building across the way. I wondered what they were working on. I wondered what they were talking about. I imagined being outside instead of inside that room. I imagined it so hard that I believed it, leaving my body in the big chair surrounded by the strange man and my parents' expired love for each other. My mind wandered in search of somebody, anybody, who might have a different reality I could join.

I believe somewhere in or around that moment, in that office, in that chair, looking out that window, it hit me what was about to happen. Everything got goofed up for a while in our family. All the sameness ended. We had no routine—no meal times or bed times or chores. There was no allowance. I had been sure it was temporary until then.

As I stared out that window, I went far inside myself. I believe fear and grief began to fully consume me. My parents didn't want me. I wasn't enough.

It sounded like I was in a wind tunnel. Everything disappeared and faded away except my laser focus on how I had to behave well. I was nine years old.

* * *

White-knuckled, I clung to his jacket as he slammed the side door of the minivan shut. His impatient patting on my back was clearly one of, "Okay, enough now. Go. Go." I tried not to look too desperate as my eyes pleaded with him to put me back in the car and take me with him.

My mother watched from the stairs, where she gathered us back after our weekends with Dad. If I looked too sad it would make

Mom sad and she'd want to talk about it. I didn't want to talk to Mom about Dad, or my stepmom or my sister, because every detail I shared broke her heart. She smiled and pretended she was happy for him and for me, but sometimes, at times like that, I felt like I could choke on her sadness; literally suffocate on all of the invisible feelings and words unspoken.

I'd skip up the steps, wave goodbye to Dad, smile at Mom, and stifle my tears. I would run up to my room, lock the door, and blare my music as high as the volume could take it. My favorite song at that time was "With a Child's Heart" by the Jackson Five. I made an audio tape of that song that repeated over and over again, on both sides so I could listen to it for hours. Michael's voice put my insides back together in place. I felt God when I heard that song. Something about it touched what felt true and I could breathe again. I'd play it and stare out the window. Heavy doses of Michael's tender and knowing voice, the innocent lyrics, and delicate leaves blowing in the wind outside, validated things I felt but couldn't see.

Music and voices are invisible, but oh so powerful; they move me. Wind is invisible, but it's real because it makes the leaves dance. These things kept me tender. They were obvious proof that even things I can't see can be significant in my life. Long before I could articulate this concept, deep down from an early age, I knew it. Music, story, wind, and trees kept me from turning to coal.

* * *

When I was young, I wrote on anything I could find. Words have leaked out of me my whole life. I'd spill them everywhere, unabashedly revealing my thoughts until I learned to contain them, gained the discipline for silence. I was eight when Dad gifted me my first journal. It may as well have been a bucket my parents bought to catch spills, and it worked. I dripped every thought, feeling, desire, and anger onto those pages. Every prayer, every feeling of confusion, or moment of happiness.

One particular happiness confessed in that journal was how much I loved my teacher. I would proclaim my love for her over and over in words or drawings I sketched. It made Mom nervous and she told me to stop saying that so much. She said it was okay to like a teacher but loving one so much was strange.

Shamefully, I went through my whole journal and added "like a sister" to every declaration of "I love my teacher". I didn't have a sister at the time, but I had brothers whom I loved a lot, so I guessed that love directed at siblings was acceptable.

Young people have so little reference from which to make sense of their lives. By default, I learned not to talk about my feelings. I crossed out every "so much" that I'd written, as in, "I love my babysitter so much." One of my most prominent childhood memories is going through that 'private' journal and editing my truth into fiction.

I've always loved so big that it nearly swallowed me whole. As a little girl I found objects, or people, of affection. There was a babysitter, a few teachers, and TV stars, too. It's always killed me how ready the world is to dote on a little boy and girl in preschool who take to each other. The adults laugh and coo at how adorable they are, and how little so-and-so has a girlfriend or boyfriend. The speculation begins about whether they will get married one day. We are so quick to pair off children into couples, suggesting we can derive more adoration as a couple than being alone.

* * *

I have always enjoyed going to school. I like learning new things and exploring information. I felt safe at school, most of the time. Twice during the elementary years there was gossip about peers who wanted to fight me. The threats were both for being teacher's pet. The nights between those days held me in terror, covers pulled up below my nose, body stiff in anticipation of a morning bus ride that never seemed to come.

Only one of those two rumors came to be true. Gratefully, when the time to fight came, I'd managed to get myself near the school bus before the crowd gathered. There was some intimidating talk by my counterpart, calling me names and letting me know I wasn't special. The crowd loved this, demonstrated by the chatter and clapping among a few. The kids who were outsiders like me at that moment, they clutched their books tightly to their chests, shoulders raised to their ears in silence, hoping I'd do something amazing to put this girl in her place and eradicate all teasing from this day forward.

The pressure was on, and I was keenly aware that while I could see the bus and its open door, a ring of students prevented me a clear path to safety. I also realized that with this many students gathered, it was only a short matter of time before the principal or a teacher would come to break it up.

The cheering and jeering had my adrenaline worked up, and while I wasn't the type to puff out my chest, I felt ready to take everything that hurt inside and hurl it at her if she got too close. She did get too close, and I felt every ounce of my past compliant behavior gather into a storm of fury. I shoved her with years of anguish, and clear across the circle she flew.

When she landed against the far side of the wall of children, it had grown silent, scores of startled eyes frozen wide, fixed on my red face that now had tears streaming down my cheeks. "LEAVE ME ALONE!" I screamed from the tips of my toes. It felt like the words and emotion behind them landed on top of her, holding her down. I stood for a moment, foreign to my own skin and power, before I quietly gathered my things and turned toward the bus. When I did, the crowd parted, and I was afforded the first choice of seats on the bus ride home that day.

As the other kids took seats around me, they jostled my shoulders and told me how cool it was to see me push the bully. Everyone wanted to congratulate me for fighting her. Had I seen the look on her face? Nobody ever stood up to her!

I wanted to be left alone. I meant what I said. I wanted to be alone. It didn't feel good that I had pushed her. It didn't feel good that I had unleashed the place where all of my anger slept. It didn't feel good that everyone thought she was a monster. We were both just girls who saw secret parts of ourselves reflected in the other. Neither of us was ready for the world to see those parts.

CHAPTER THREE

Any chance I got I would skip recess and stay inside to sit with my favorite teacher in a quiet classroom, grading papers. The open windows permitted all of the screaming and shouting from the playground in, but it was muffled, distant. It wasn't my chaos to worry about, like the noise of a train passing over faraway tracks, going somewhere away from me.

I felt seen by Ms. Belser. She was my fifth-grade teacher, and she was the only person on the planet when I was ten years old that I felt fully safe around. Hindsight says I had a crush on her that, by definition, insisted I be near her whenever possible. I could let down all of my guards. I knew that anything that threatened me while she was around, she would deal with it. She would shut it down.

One of the things I loved about Ms. Belser is that it wasn't only me that she protected. She had a way of protecting all of the small people in her classroom. She protected us from the world, and from each other. She was a leader, a mediator, a referee. She had the power to throw one of us out of the room or to the principal's office if we didn't comply. I was safe in a structure that she controlled, and I looked forward to the routine of her class. She seemed tall and powerful to me. It was the eighties, and she wore big chunky earrings and bracelets to decorate sharp, often one-piece dresses. She didn't wear lace or bunched sleeves or belts. Her dresses were simple in style, and bold in colors. She always wore high heels, make-up, and her hair was done perfectly every day. I admired how she put herself together; Ms. Belser was beautiful like my mother, but different. She was fancier than Mom, and she had dark black skin. I fantasized that I might grow up to be like her. She was smart and confident, in charge. She had the most beautiful handwriting and I loved to watch her teach. There was nothing she didn't know.

I was attracted to powerful women. There were many at that school. Teachers who were wise and commanding. Black women who seemed to run things. I wanted to be like them. In all of my daydreams about being an adult, I started to notice that I was imagining myself as a beautiful black woman with style and power. As the impossibility of my becoming such an adult was clear, another layer of conscious discomfort emerged—wearing fair skin. This was a self-perceived shortcoming she never shamed me about. I always felt like I held great possibility in Ms. Belser's presence.

From time to time, my dad would drop me off late and I'd have to open the classroom door, disturbing a lesson as I got to my seat. While I was hot with embarrassment and felt like everybody was staring at me, I soon remembered that I was finally safe in class, in a seat that belonged to me. Even in my absence, no one else would sit there because it was mine. I had a place that I didn't need to defend or justify. My name was on the roster. My role was student. My teacher was in charge. My job was to learn. It was all very clear. Clarity was welcome and appreciated.

Once I stayed after school to help Ms. Belser grade papers, and when we were done, I called home for a ride. Nobody answered and my teacher decided to drive me home. I was on top of the world that my realities were about to merge. My teacher would see where I lived, and maybe one day she would come and take me away.

Her car smelled like cigarettes from an overflowing ash tray in the front seat. She asked me to sit in the back. She told me that she smoked cigarettes and it was a bad habit. She hoped I would make better decisions than she had. I told her I didn't mind. I told her my mom smoked cigarettes, too. She was asking about my homework when I saw her look in the rear-view mirror and say something under her breath. Then I heard a siren blip a few times and I felt scared inside.

"Everything's okay, Jenny. Just be quiet and sit still, okay?" I did as she asked.

An officer came to the window and asked her a question. She shuffled around in her front seat and handed him something, then looking straight ahead. The tension was familiar somehow, and I held all of my questions and concerns. I bit the inside of my cheeks to stay quiet like she'd asked, but suddenly I wanted to take care of her. Her energy felt different than I'd ever felt from her before. It felt like she needed protection, but I sat still. She lit a cigarette.

The officer returned to her door and asked her to step out of the car. I almost blurted out, "Where are you taking her!?" but I honored her instructions instead. I was afraid, frozen. Once she was out of the car, I got up on my knees and turned around to see them talking by his car. Two white officers stood facing her, one with his arms crossed. She had her hands behind her back, and she was nodding to the second officer whose hands were pointing to me in her car. Was he speaking to her, or screaming? She would begin to speak and then stop. Begin, get cut off, and stop. She looked over and saw my eyes reading the moment. I wondered, why was she acting that way? I had never seen her like this. My powerhouse teacher was submissive.

The talkative officer got back in their patrol car and it looked like he was on a phone talking to someone. His eyes stayed affixed to

Ms. Belser and he was nodding his head. The other officer stood sternly with arms crossed, not speaking. He looked like he was a guard, but I didn't know what he was guarding. Ms. Belser didn't move.

Suddenly the two men in uniform were smiling and laughing; it looked like they were trying to be nice, but my teacher didn't look amused. She looked small next to the officers, until her arm came away from her body and she pointed back toward me in the car, too. I watched her suddenly remember who she was, and I saw her inflate to the woman I admired. She reached out her hand to the officers who each shook it one at a time. She smiled politely and then she marched back to the car. Her eyes immediately caught mine and her hand made a hidden motion, in front of her body, that only I could see. It told me to turn around and sit down. NOW.

The rest of the car ride home was quiet, and I could feel a change in her. There were no words for the moment. None that I could find. She helped by saying, under her breath but loud enough so I could hear, "A black woman can't drive a white child home from school without looking like a kidnapper!" I was confused. "Why did the police think you were kidnapping me?"

I heard her take a deep breath. Twice. Her exhale was loud and slow. When we pulled over in front of my house, Ms. Belser stretched her arm across the front seat and turned to look at me. "Jenny, do you know what the word adversity means?" I was happy she was talking to me, relieved that I didn't have to peel myself out of the thick silence we'd been sitting in.

"No."

"Adversity means, difficulties. Hard stuff. The kind of stuff that hurts your heart. Do you know what that is?"

It took me a moment to answer because I needed to wrap my head around it.

There is a word for the way I feel?

"Yes, I do know what that is."

"I know you do, Jenny. Now you listen to me." Her eyes were stern but warm, and her red fingernail was pointing at me to drive her thought home. Whatever she was about to say was meant to stick. I gave her every ounce of my attention.

"Jenny, you have a light inside of you, a special light, like a bright flame on a candle. Adversity will try to extinguish that. Adversity will try to blow that light out."

I knew what she was talking about.

"You promise me, Jennifer. Promise me that no matter what, you won't let that light inside of you go out. You got to shine."

I wanted to climb over the seat and hug her. I wanted to thank her for saying words that stitched my two worlds together. My insides and the outside. I couldn't believe that she knew exactly what I needed.

"Are you okay? Did those policemen give you adversity?" She chuckled and puckered her lips into a face that she made when she got a kick out of me. "They try, baby, but I got a light, too, and they can't have it."

I was so glad. I loved her light.

"Jenny, promise me." I saw my mother descending our front steps and walking toward the car. I didn't want to leave this pocket of truth.

"I promise."

"Okay now, baby. Your mom's come to get you. I'll see you in class. Be good."

My mother bent down and waved to my teacher as I ran into the house, determined to get to my room and close the door so I could continue to marinate in Ms. Belser's confidence and acknowledgment. When I got to the top of the stairs, I looked down and Mom was leaning in the passenger window, talking with my teacher. Grateful, I closed the door.

* * *

A year later I stood next to Ms. Belser as the bell rang on my last day of sixth grade. I was moving to another town for junior high and I didn't know if I'd ever see her again. My throat was tight with emotion and she held an energetic conversation with the principal. I wanted to pull on her jacket, I wanted to jump up and down, I'd do anything to get her attention. I also didn't want her stern reprimand upon me. "Jennifer are you crazy? Act like you have some sense!" I decided I better not miss the bus, so I left. I had cinderblocks on my feet as I stepped away from her, trudging down the stairs and through the corridor of memories to abandon it all and become the new girl again. The bus door was closed when I got outside so I screamed and waved my arms at the driver.

The hydraulic doors whispered open and landed with a pop! to welcome me aboard. Panting, I found a seat by the window. I scanned the yard outside in case she ran outside to say goodbye to me. But she hadn't come. I suppose she didn't even notice that I was gone.

The bus made all of its sputtering and clanking noises that set it into motion, and I heard the door shut. I stared at the dark green bus seat in front of me and my throat gripped me tighter, forcing tears from my eyes. For a moment as we pulled away from the school, I felt like I might explode, but something strange happened. It was like a switch was flipped and the tears stopped. One sniff and I packed it away. I made a decision that day that I didn't need anybody.

* * *

On one level, I still trusted the safety I felt hanging out with God. In spite of the hostility people attributed to Him, or the contrast I'd witnessed as a Preacher's Kid (PK) between home and church, I knew God was good. But it felt like God had gone with Dad. I missed them both. To bring up God was to remind us of Dad and vice versa. This is where I began to let go of belonging to a church or having conversations with people as if God loved me. When my parents split and all of our friendships split, too, I started to feel like I was on the outside looking in, and that included my relationship with God. I felt ashamed of being separated from a world where we had been together as a family. A schism was born inside of me and I couldn't reconcile my discouraged heart about God. I feared He was disappointed in me, like I had no longer had any right to him. That loss mirrored my feelings of having less right to my father when he remarried. Everything around me had changed so absolutely, and I just went with it. What choice did I have? Eventually, alcohol helped.

My friend Ann had an older brother, Christopher. I lived in the first house, and Ann and Christopher lived in the last house on the same block. There were nearly twenty houses and yards between us, and thanks to the ground we could cover on our bikes, we became best friends. We spent a lot of time in each other's homes and her parents became like my parents and mine like hers. Even after mine divorced, I'd hang out at Ann's place on weekends when I visited Dad. She and I shared a lot in common. We both loved video games, pickles, office supplies, and riding bikes. We both had older brothers and we both had parents who kept cigarettes and beer around. At Dad's house, those things were mostly out of sight. At Ann's place, it was as simple as opening the refrigerator.

The first time I remember drinking alcohol was in the basement at Ann's house, when her brother and my brother were hanging out. They weren't friends per se, but they were close in age and there were mutual friends around the neighborhood who would go to Ann and Christopher's house to drink, smoke, play video games, and shoot pool. We had to stuff fresh, laundered socks into the pool table pockets so the balls wouldn't make noise. Ann's mom was usually watching her soap operas upstairs, and her dad didn't want us 'fucking around' with his pool table. He took great pride in it. Since we didn't listen, we adjusted.

One of the times that I was there, the older kids were standing on their heads against the wall and drinking beer from a mug. They were drinking upside down! Our friend Tony did it like most everything else he ever attempted, with great ease. I thought it would be easy and I always wanted to impress Tony. He was my brother's best friend and I wanted him to notice me. I tried to do the handstand and drink beer, but suffice it to say, I failed miserably. I got beer in my nose and proceeded to be consumed with choking fits for a half hour. The older kids laughed at me and called me names.

I had managed to get some beer in my mouth and felt a warmth over my body that I'd never experienced before. I was standing in the noise of the basement and felt calmer than ever before. The baseball game was on, music was playing, all of the neighborhood kids were laughing and cussing and talking over each other, and I felt fine. None of it was bothering me. I had never realized how much the noise overwhelmed me.

I walked over to the small basement refrigerator where the beer was kept and got my own. It was Stroh's. It was cold. I pulled back the tab and it spit at me. It smelled awful. I took a few big gulps and noticed how things around me seemed even calmer. I burped. I smiled. It was magic.

We moved several times between grade school and the high school I'd graduate from. In those days, instead of church, we slept in on Sundays. Mom still prayed with us at bedtime, but I didn't see her as much because she worked two, sometimes three jobs. I acquired a layer of "oh well" to my tween attitude, but it was a mask. I was tangled up inside unless I was pretending to be on stage. My friends and I would dance around and lip sync to the Annie and Mary Poppins albums. I wanted to be on *Saturday Night Live* one day, like Gilda Radner and Jane Curtin. I knew life didn't feel this way for performers. The fantasy of becoming famous manifested. It allowed me to escape to a happy place where I could be anyone I wanted to be.

I'd come to see a clear lack of congruence between the words spoken in public by believers and the way that they lived their lives in private. I saw people harmed by the actions of Christians. By the time I was able to identify crushes for peers or teachers, I was more interested in Boy George and Michael Jackson than God and His church. There seemed far too many problems with the way people treated each other to buy into the sort of Christianity of intolerance being peddled by the people I saw. I preferred my private, personal friend whom I trusted and told everything to. I told God all about my love interests, and the good and bad feelings that went along with discovering my sexual orientation and interest in intimacy.

I was turned off by Christianity as I knew it, and I thought that mere fact alone made me bad. I'd learned, in theory, what was right and wrong but rarely seen it lived. It was a tragic reality for me, that my lived experience was something I'd been taught to either doubt or completely ignore, to survive.

A young girl separated from her intuition is a tragic thing, because I had acquired too much information that was in conflict with my heart. I couldn't be all of me and didn't trust myself to decide which parts were okay when, and with whom. My youth was an exercise in separating fact from fiction, truth from translation. I knew that the noise outside of me had become too loud, and that holding secrets had added shame to my experience. I wanted to expose my pure, honest wishes and dreams to the light of day, but feared unforeseen consequences. I had so little foundation for trusting myself; my need to belong was stronger than my faith in God and myself. It felt safer to live on the surface as though right in the eyes of others, rather than be true to what felt right to me. I had learned to restrain what was natural to me. I kept my thoughts and feelings on lockdown.

I would spend years reaching for things outside of myself to take the edge off my own imbalance. I never learned to justify or be at peace with living on the common beliefs of others, the system of behavior I had been given, instead of the genuine faith and values I had developed through personal experience. I couldn't (and still can't) extricate myself from my life or live only parts of myself. All of me is true. Aligning myself internally took serious effort and presenting myself to the world often became too much. I grew withdrawn and stayed locked in my room or put on a mask and made people laugh.

* * *

It was a warm, sunny day under a clear blue sky. Several manned grills produced smoke smelling of ribs and chicken, burgers and brats. It was the mid-eighties and the oldies station played from a two-speaker boom box on one end of a picnic table. I was twelve years old. We were at my aunt's house, celebrating a niece's christening. It was an awkward time in my life; I was adjusting to a new town. My mom had remarried into this family and I'd just started junior high. I didn't have many friends, felt like an outcast, and I was wondering why I was supposed to call all of these strangers my family.

It was then, during a game of lawn darts, that I happened to see my brother's girlfriend grab a beer out of a nearby cooler. I knew she wasn't old enough to drink; she was only a sophomore in high school. I didn't think much of it until, over the course of a few games, I noticed other people retrieve drinks, too. I was thirsty and decided that after this game, I would head over there to see if there was water or pop.

There I was, winning a game of lawn darts against some older guy in his mid-twenties, and I was suddenly overcome with a full body warmth and tingle as I remembered the beer I'd had in Ann's basement. Everything had been fine until I remembered that drink. Then it was all I could think about. Remembering the calm that followed that beer was on my mind. All of the reasons I was uncomfortable shot to the foreground, and I excused myself from the game to find my brother's girlfriend. I talked her into getting me a beer, and she decided a wine cooler was a better choice for me. I thanked her and went to drink it in hiding behind the shed, to see if the effect would be the same as I remembered. It tasted like Kool-Aid, and I felt better than I remembered. I also had the confidence to walk to the cooler and grab a second without assistance.

As that afternoon of drinking continued, the quality of my balance and speech declined. I learned a game called Quarters and failed miserably at getting my coin into the cup. I believe I missed on purpose at first, waiting to hear the blessed cry, "Drink!"

The next day I awoke in my aunt's bathtub. It was the only bathroom in the house, and I'd been sitting in it for more than sixteen hours, passed out. I had vomit on my shirt and in my hair, and I felt like I was going to die. The whole world and its noise felt disconnected and painfully intrusive.

When I saw my mother at the door, she had her hands on her hips and pity in her eyes. "Good morning." She shook her head and came into the bathroom, sat on the toilet, and asked how I was feeling. The air between us sounded muffled, like the sound of an old 45 of a Billie Holiday recording. There were no knobs to tune it in or make the volume lower. I squinted my eyes at Mom and wondered what had happened.

This is what I learned: She said I'd become very sick last night, sneaking drinks. I'd thrown up all over my aunt's bedroom like The Exorcist movie. My mom had come in and tried to clean up after me, but I began screaming and swinging my arms at her, saying ugly things. Someone came to put me in the bathtub so Mom could wash me off, but by the time I fell in the tub, they were tired of the struggle. I passed out and people continued to use the bathroom around me for the remainder of the night.

I was listening and wondering why I couldn't remember any of that. The main reason I wouldn't argue Mom's story was because I didn't have the energy. The thought of using words hurt my brain, and I could smell the evidence of her tale in my hair. While I have to, in good conscience, say that I was disgusted with myself, I believe that is in hindsight only. At that moment I realized that I felt nothing of the awkwardness from the day before I drank, I remembered nothing about the unpleasant events Mom described, and I sat, awestruck that I had truly found something magical. I hiccupped and smiled. Alcohol could help me disappear.

CHAPTER FOUR

High school is where a lot of things started to change. I was desperately interested in fitting in and having friends, as I always felt so alone. An adorable and courageous sophomore approached me in the bleachers at one of our first football games. I was sitting by myself in denim from head to toe, accented by my wildly feathered blonde hair. Javier was an athlete and a dancer, an artist and a mama's boy.

Javier is the boy I fell in love with. We went to parties and we watched The Little Mermaid and other Disney animated films together. His family welcomed me; his tiny mother, Maria, showed me love and embraced me into the family. I felt the safest I'd ever felt since my life had been turned upside down at ten years old. I trusted Javier, enjoyed being with him, and experienced my first sex with him. I was completely invested and felt good about it. My mom liked him, too.

That relationship with Javier and his family was a new experience and I thrived in it. I craved the attention and affection Javier gave me. His family was somewhat like mine—they had their problems, but they loved each other. He was funny, and we made each other laugh. I wanted to keep him and the way he looked at me, hold onto the way I felt safe in his arms. I loved him, no doubt. He had told me he loved me, and all our friends knew. I liked feeling special that way. I loved the attention we got as a couple, how validated I felt by our peers because I was with him. People would coo about how hot he was and how sweet we were together. I felt, for the first time, like I belonged.

No peace ever lasted long in my young life. Soon, all was sent into chaos again when I developed a distracting interest in a girl named Zanni in my math class. She sat behind me and pulled at my hair enough times that I finally had to turn around. Our introduction consisted of me whisper-yelling, "Would you please stop doing that!?" Her smirking face studied me as she shifted down into her seat. Her lips were pink, and her eyes were large and round, framed by long brown hair and a dimple to boot. An unexpected shiver ran through me. She informed me in a husky whisper that she may need some help, or that maybe she could help me. Her eyes settled on her pencil eraser as she bounced it against the desk nervously— she was blushing. The first time we spoke she was playful and flirtatious. She looked anywhere but my eyes when she called me smart and pretty. She smelled like Lady Stetson and Marlboro Reds and I couldn't stop thinking about her. I would do my hair and make-up in the morning for her. I'd go to school motivated but not to go to any classes, hoping to catch a glimpse of Zanni in the hallway. I prayed that she would pass me a note, and maybe our hands would touch. Maybe the note would smell like her, maybe she'd smile at me. I could hold her handwriting in my pocket, anything.

The way I felt for her and the way I felt for Javier were starkly different. I wanted to keep the bubble Javier and I had created together in my messy world, and I started to feel awful as my feelings for the girl kidnapped my focus. I couldn't seem to help myself. I'd be weird with him because I couldn't make sense of why I felt so different with her. I began to wonder if he felt toward me the way I felt toward him, or the way I felt toward her. When I did think about him there was tremendous guilt, because I believe he felt for me what I felt for her. I'd change plans with him to spend time with her.

Sometimes I'd sleep over at her house and we'd go to bed at 8:00 p.m. just so we could be alone. We would stay up until midnight not talking or touching, but lying in her bed listening to music, staring at each other. The words dared not be spoken, but neither one of us wanted to be anywhere else in the world. I'd tap my hand on the bed between us, as if really enjoying the music, and from time to time she'd stop my hand with hers and I burned so fiercely that I could hardly meet her eyes. She'd hold my hand just a little longer than necessary, but we said nothing. *After all, each of us had boyfriends.*

One night during a sleepover, the sensation was so intense that touching hands was not enough. She shuffled her body slightly towards me and I panicked, hardly able to breathe. I flipped my body over so that I was facing away from her. It was too much, and I didn't know what else to do. I wanted her to wrap herself around me so badly, to attach to me, and after an excruciating period of time, she did. I stared straight ahead and held her hands around me tight and she pulled herself into me, spooning me from behind. We lay like that until I felt her head, which had been tucked into my neck, begin working its way around to my face to look at me. I couldn't face her. I just wanted to feel this way forever, so I closed my eyes.

I was fourteen when Zanni and I first kissed. There was no fancy Hollywood head bobbing side to side, there was no dramatic tongue or anything. She simply placed her closed lips on my closed lips, and we stayed there in an absolute fever. It sent chills through my entire body and I froze as I blushed. Eventually, I opened my eyes to find hers closed. I took note of the details of her handsome and beautiful face. I studied her eyelashes and the shape of her eyes. I felt like the luckiest girl in the world to be wrapped up in her smell and even in her fully clothed body, I didn't want it ever to end. The whole world could burn to the ground in that moment and I wouldn't have noticed. It was the most soft and exciting connection I'd ever felt—safe and terrifying and tender, all at the same time.

One day I waited by the water fountain that she and I would meet at between classes so long that the bell rang, and I was alone in the hallway, late for class. I heard gym shoes squeaking in the distance and I knew it was her—I had a Pavlov's response to those squeaks. We played on the JV basketball team together and I'd learned the sounds of her running on the waxed floor. She whipped around the corner, out of breath and her face broke into a smile. "You're still here! And wearing that sweater that I love." She noticed. "Here, I'm sorry I'm late. Can you come over tonight after school?" She handed me a note and I confirmed that I'd see her after school. She smiled and tore around the corner to her class. I chuckled at all of the noise her Nike made, and my heart was full. I took a deep breath and calculated that I wouldn't be able to read her letter for another hour if I went to class, so I ditched class and went to the library instead. Her words on paper were burning a hole in my palm but I waited until I got far in the back of the stacks, so I'd be far enough from people to allow myself an emotional response to her words. When I was alone, I put my books down and unfolded her letter, which was half a page long, handwritten. Always in pencil.

Hey, Little One. I'm sitting in this boring class and I think the clock is broke cuz it's taking forever for class to end. I wonder if you could come over tonight after practice. I might have to clean but I want to be with you. Even if Moms is around and we can't be alone, I feel better when you're close to me. You're one in a million and I wanted to write a quick note to tell you I think so. Yep. That's it! I'll try to get this to you by the water fountain, but I gotta go drop something off to coach so I might not make it. Anyways, I can't wait to see your face.

It began to gnaw at me that I was not being honest with Javier—I never meant to lie, but I'd never had this experience to learn from. I was just finding my way, one day at a time. I adored my boyfriend and didn't want to hurt him. I liked his attention and his notes and drawings and kisses, but it wasn't the same. I didn't want to keep him from finding someone capable of sharing the feelings he had for me. The feelings I felt toward her.

In 1978, two very important things happened. My baby brother Bo was born in July, and a movie that would affirm and therefore change my life, was released in November. While I don't believe I saw the film until I was in high school, it starred Gena Rowlands (Linda Ray), Jane Alexander (Barbara Moreland) and a young Nancy McKeon (Susan Moreland). It was titled *A Question of Love* and was based on the true story of a woman fighting her ex-husband for custody of her youngest son because she was in a relationship with another woman.

The film named many of the prejudices that surround same-sex love. Both women were beautiful and that alone contradicted everything I'd imagined could be true for lesbians. In hindsight, all points of view were offered with equanimity and I sat nearly nose-to-screen watching. The volume was as low as it would play and still allow me to hear it. They were saying words I didn't want anyone in my family to overhear, or they would want to know why I was watching it.

That movie felt like a lifeline, and those characters were the first sighting of land to a girl who'd been adrift, wondering if the weight of my truth might cause me to drown. Characters in the film said all the things I'd learned I shouldn't speak or ask about. Nearly ten minutes into the story, Gena and her oldest son had an honest conversation, and I was hooked. I was both her son with the questions, and the mother with no answers.

Nearly fifteen minutes into the movie, Linda Ray's mother told her how she felt. It crushed Linda to have her own mother calling her perverted and disgusting. I watched Linda's character crumble in heartache at her mother's words, but she still took up for herself. I'd never even considered that an option—that my perspective or experience may have a seat at the table. Until that moment I had been convinced that the world and the Bible and my parents and hatred were in the right, and I was therefore bad and confused and in the wrong. I shouldn't expose my badness, lest I be judged harshly.

An invisible moat had somehow formed between my real self and the me I gave to the world. I'd abandoned authenticity years before, to become a chameleon. Jenny was a girl who had learned to change color in any circumstance, to be the most pleasing in order to belong.

✳ ✳ ✳

My mother often came into my room after work or before she went to sleep. Sometimes she'd sing to me, sometimes we'd chat, and whenever she could she would come to say she loved me, fluff the blankets around me, and kiss me goodnight. One of those nights I was burning to tell somebody about my friend from math class.

I wanted desperately to talk about it, to ask someone to explain it to me! I'd become obsessed and secretly looked for Zanni around every corner. I didn't know who to ask except my mother, but I was anxious because I recalled the editing of my journals and sensed this was something she'd tell me to scratch out. I knew, though. I knew I did not love Zanni like a sister.

I was prepared to ask Mom outright, if kissing a friend was okay, because that's what had happened. I figured the worst possible result would be Mom having a horrible reaction, but at least I'd know. I needed to know. I never felt this way when Javier kissed me.

When Mom came into my room and sat on the edge of my bed that night, she moved the hair out of my face to see me clearly. I said, "Mom, can I ask you a question?" Something in the way the next few seconds played out had me lose my courage to be forthright, and I found myself asking if it was weird to like it when a good friend holds your hand. She studied me for a second and then stood up. Her energy didn't match her words as she kissed my forehead and said something like, "Of course, it's good to have friends you love. Girlfriends are a lot of fun!"

I've always wondered if Mom's quick exit was manufactured by me, because I like to think she knew I was different, but never intended to discuss it. I don't know if my recollection of a lot of that time is accurate, but I do know I learned at a young age not to trust my perception of the world I lived in. I lay in bed, certain Mom was grateful that I hadn't asked about a kiss on the lips, even if it had been the most divine of moments, the most innocent connection between two young girls that created an electric storm in my stomach and my chest. I was pretty sure I would keep this experience to myself.

Sometime after that evening, Mom invited me to take a seat with her in the back yard. I was probably fifteen at the time, and already smoking cigarettes, mostly Mom's cigarettes. I was skeptical of her invitation when she offered me a beer. Alcohol had always been around our home, and I was known to sneak into it from time to time, or drink with my friends. Drinking with my mom in the back yard on a Saturday was a scenario I'd not found myself in before. I was concerned that something had happened and asked if she was okay. She assured me that she was.

My mother has one of the biggest hearts I know. She was hurting for years, and I was self-centered and made it harder for her, yet she consistently stepped out of the mess to love me. Mom was raised in a chivalrous world. Her grandparents had adored each other, and the dynamic between them fed Mom's dreams of what marriage would be. Through her eyes, grandpa drove, paid for, and doted on his wife, leaving her to manage the household and family tasks that women were encouraged toward at that time. Mom wanted and expected to be cared for and appreciated in the same way, so that became the job of my father when she married him at nineteen. Their mothers were both in the church choir, and for all I know their relationship may have been match-made. They were both attractive, from good church families, and single. They stayed married for fifteen years.

As life unfolds people grow and their needs can change. My parents had three children together before they grew in parallel directions. Ultimately, the relationship dissolved. When my mom found herself solo, we kids were her reason to press on. She had only ever wanted to be a wife and mother; by her own admission, that was her dream. She is also an artist; she can do anything creative, and loves making personalized, unique gifts for Christmas and birthdays. She doesn't enjoy taking risks; is mostly pleased with the simple things like family, her garden, and crafts. But my mother has a remarkable amount of courage, faith, and patience, as well as, I suspect, hurt. It always seemed to me that she was alone, without a support system to help her grieve life's disappointments.

The church failed to hold her after the divorce; not because she didn't want to go. I believe it was too painful for her, as it had become for me, but for different reasons. We both had too many ghosts inside of any sanctuary. But my mother never let go of God. She always prayed with us and encouraged us to love God. We simply learned God outside of the building. Church wasn't about God anymore. It had become a funhouse of distorted mirrors and hypocrisy, a battleground for the family, a tug of war for friends and favor. We had lost too much there.

My mother made mistakes, many of which she owns today, but Mom's arms, Mom's couch, and Mom's ear were reliable. She was a refuge even when things got complicated with divorce and alcohol and adolescence. She raised my brothers and me like so many women do—left to play both roles of provider and nurturer. This was well outside of Mom's comfort zone, as it was for many women in her generation, and with far too many eyes judging them. Mom was also without her father to turn to, whom she had loved dearly. He died in her mid-twenties and she had been Daddy's girl, his first daughter. That may have been the first of many deep breaks her heart would endure. She changed after losing him. It alters a tribe when the leader departs. Everyone must reimagine themselves and their roles.

We both sat silently in our yard, facing the brick grill and the alley behind. This was a good location for a private chat. Distance between us and the house meant less chance anyone might hear our conversation.

The silence was pregnant with tension and with love—I could feel that her words and next steps were being carefully scrutinized before she spoke. I was anxious to know what was happening, but aimed to follow her lead, and knew she was looking for the words to begin. I trusted her love for me, so I waited. Afraid.

Finally, she broke the silence and asked how Javier and I were doing. I told her I'd broken up with him, and she wanted to know what happened. When I didn't respond she asked, "Does it have anything to do with your feelings for girls?" We each had a beer to lubricate the conversation she had no blueprint for. She was dying to know who her little girl was becoming. I think she was afraid to know the truth, and also to not know. When I spoke to her about my feelings for Zanni, we both stared straight ahead. She said she never had that experience, so she couldn't relate. I asked her that day not to tell anyone, because I had to date guys and stay in the closet at school.

We wouldn't discuss my sexuality again until two years later, when I was sitting on the couch watching TV with my senior prom date,

Corban. That was the night she asked me to tell my big brother Josh the secret I'd asked her to keep.

I was vaguely aware of my older brother, Josh, who was graduating high school; and my younger brother, Bo, who was finishing the sixth grade. I mostly felt alone. Soon Josh would begin working and Bo would move to another state and become a part of my father's new family. The stories Josh and I shared about our dad weren't great stories, and that information conflicted with what Bo saw, which was stability and a sober man. It appealed to him. He needed to see for himself.

My father had a new son and a new daughter, a new wife and a new life. It would be years before I was willing or able to move anywhere near touching that hurt. I had too much on my plate. With my little brother Bo leaving, Mom struggled to let go of her youngest. She knew he wanted to know his dad better and didn't want to keep him from that, but it was hard for her to watch him leave.

Fortunately, she'd found a man who took good care of her, and we liked him, too.

During the week, Mom worked long hours at two minimum wage jobs to keep us sheltered and fed in a beautiful house. She would drink at home or go to the bar with her boyfriend some nights after work. My mother endured scrutiny from many directions, having gone through divorce. But she was beautiful and smart and creative, and she loved us so much that it suffocated me sometimes.

For many reasons, codependency in a broken family system is detrimental to the development of children. That said, I've learned to take the good with the bad. I believe that feeling emotionally responsible for my mother gave me purpose during some of my darkest hours. I couldn't in good conscience imagine hurting myself and her finding me that way—without me there to hold her through it.

God works in mysterious ways.

CHAPTER FIVE

L ife didn't pan out where I started high school in West Chicago, so we moved again. In Elmhurst, IL, halfway through my sophomore year, I was consumed in grief and gathering courage to start over yet again.

When I arrived at my second high school, I knew my strengths and weaknesses. I was pretty, funny, smart, and athletic. I was also gay, and for the first time I'd be going to a school that was primarily white. I don't know which scared me more, being around so many white people or having to stay in the closet for three more years. A part of me was grateful for a new start; the other part was devastated after being extracted from vital relationships in my life. I arrived in the middle of sophomore year exhausted, but with a developed and appealing persona. I had crafted my mask with care. I'd found alcohol and the closet to bridge the distance between church folks and myself. I was in the closet and intended to stay there.

What began after the divorce, was solidified by the time I was sixteen years old. I'd lost complete interest in the church for two main reasons. First, I chose to let go of my father, and to do that I had to stop going to church. There were far too many ghosts of another life in the pews, a life that was no longer mine. Second, I had gathered, in no uncertain terms, where I was welcome as a queer person and where I wasn't. Church felt like a pretty clear 'not welcome'.

I stopped entertaining the idea of ever returning to a brick and mortar church— someone had to be on Mom's team. She had lost the ability to sit in church, and she had lost her friends, too. No matter. I had preferred my private conversations with God since I was little.

God for me in those days took on the role of a midnight counselor—someone I would cry out to through the pages of my notebooks. God had become something of a caretaker who would tuck me in after I'd been shuffling through the world, when I was angry with how it worked, disappointed in how people were treated, and afraid to be myself. Often drunk or high, I would detail the day's events in nearly illegible scribble, feeling at times victorious and others, defeated. It seemed that the more I drank the more I needed to drink, and it became anyone's guess whether I'd feel the relief or not. Regardless, I drank as much as I could whenever I could. My body begged for it like needing water in a desert. Drunk, I would cry out to God with my pen and eventually, pity myself to sleep.

* * *

Corban had come over to watch TV. He was a hockey player; tall, Greek, and handsome. A sweetheart and a real catch. I liked him. We made a good-looking couple, and we had fun together. The problem was that I knew something he didn't know when we started dating. At that time in my life I still dated guys to distract people's attention from my desire for girls.

Usually a merkin, or beard, is a willing participant. To my knowledge, Corban didn't know he was acting as my disguise. I was in love with Zanni, but I genuinely liked him...it was all very confusing at the time. I knew that after prom, we were over, and I knew that was cruel, but not unprecedented. It began in Hollywood in the 20s when top box office actors lead personal lives contrary to the moral climate of the country. Leading ladies and cowboys don't sell films if the world knows they're gay. To nurture the illusion that some handsome gay male or seductress female actor was fodder for the heterosexual public's fantasies, gay people would parade around town to media-covered events with somebody of the opposite gender on their arm. To not do so would be career suicide, as average ticket-buying men would not go to action flicks where the dude they wanted to emulate was a 'faggot'. To not have a beautiful woman to reinforce the delusion that the star was heterosexual and therefore worthy of admiration, was dangerous.

For a woman who identified as queer in Hollywood, like anywhere else, if she was beautiful by straight men's standards, she was "safe" as long as men could have sex with her—or watch her have sex with her girlfriend.

She may have been safe as long as men were allowed to flirt and attract her attention for their ego. A man's physical strength made the situation vulnerable and it could only take a second for this game to get personal for him, if he felt he was truly being forbidden her fruit. Situations that began as 'innocent' flirting could quickly turn hostile if a man felt his socialized position was being threatened. Sometimes, in my experience, to avoid it becoming violent, a lesbian (or any woman), may resignedly submit to sex she doesn't desire, so the drama can end quickly.

Some popular terms still in use, and what they mean:

Beard—a slang term describing a person who is used, knowingly or unknowingly, as a date, romantic partner, or spouse to conceal one's sexual orientation. It's usually used to describe a woman covering for a man.

Merkin—same as a beard, referring to a man covering for a woman. Both beard and merkin imply a form of disguise.

Documentation of queer people being beaten or killed in brutal ways began around

---

[1]https://tmblr.co/ZcOIAy1MBq1_9, Hollywood's Shameful (Ongoing) History: "Beards," "Merkins," "Lavender Marriages," and the Glass Closet

1969. The public discourse did not include this topic, ever. That said, if you were queer, you heard about it. You may know about cases like Rebecca Wight and Claudia Brenner. I was haunted by stories of Brandon Teena, Matthew Shepard, and U.S. Navy Petty Officer Allen Schindler. For me, and many others, these potential realities lurk in the unspoken space between myself and everyone I choose to trust and let into my life.

If who I am threatens you, everything could change in an instant if it becomes public knowledge. The fear of such unpredictable violence kept my hair long, my nails painted, and a male by my side in most public situations. I lived multiple lives, two of which were distinguished by my sexual orientation. The face the public saw was a pretty, smart, charismatic, heterosexual tomboy girl who got along with everyone. The self that lived inside was literally on edge every minute of every day, grieving the idea of me others loved, engulfed in flames of shame that I was failing the people I loved by denying the façade they were invested in. I was always asking God to please make me 'normal'. I was paralyzed with worry that I'd misstep and get disowned, beaten, or raped.

Bisexual wasn't on my radar yet as a legitimate option, so it troubled me a bit that I liked Corban so much. As a lesbian, I thought I was supposed to be grossed out by men, that kissing them should make my stomach turn. That may be true for some gay women, but that wasn't the case for me. The men I chose to date were fine. The ones who climbed on and off me while I lay still so it would end quickly, well, I can't imagine any woman likes that if she's honest. It doesn't feel good when a man comes at you all worked up, anxiously penetrates and hammers into you until he explodes, and then rolls off of you. No one wants to be a human sperm receptacle. I don't believe disliking that had anything to do with my sexual orientation.

Ultimately, I was blinded by my feelings for Zanni, so I made sense of things as I could with the limited life experience I had. I decided that I wouldn't sleep with Corban. He liked me a lot too, and it was bad enough I was using him as my merkin to complete my senior year with as little drama as possible. I determined that with this one last high school dance under my belt, I'd be free to explore these feelings off in a city somewhere. I could finally go and discover myself when I was no longer under my mother's suburban roof.

That particular day, my mom had taken Josh out to the bar, to celebrate his twenty-first birthday. When they arrived home, they were both drunk—they'd had a nice time. I was happy to see them spending time together, but Corban and I had been having a nice afternoon until they got there.

My brother Josh was passing out on the couch and my mother had found a spot on the floor between Corban and the TV, facing Josh. She began to call to him in a whisper, oblivious to Corban and me. "Josshhh-ua. Pssst! Josshh-ua. Wake up! Your sister has something to tell you. Josshhua."

"Mom, please. We're watching this show, I can hear you." I grabbed Corban's hand to confirm that I was embarrassed, and that this was stupid, and he met my face with raised eyebrows and a controlled smirk. He had great expressions that made me laugh.

"Don't shush me, I'm your mother! I have to wake your brother so you can tell him your secret. It's only fair that you tell someone else. Who am I supposed to talk to? Tell your brother. Jossssshhhh-ua!"

Her eyes had gone stern. My whole body was hot. I could feel the heat shooting up through my ears. My mother was trying to out me in front of my prom date. She wanted me to tell my brother that I'm gay, and she was going to do it drunk in front of my date.

Fortunately, I'd become quite practiced in appearing calm while in distress, so I leaned over and told Corban we could finish the date another time, and I would walk him to his truck. He smiled and agreed.

I returned to the living room scared to death that my mom was going to make the moment happen right then, while I was completely sober. Josh and I already didn't talk or hang out as much as I would have liked to. I always lived in a state of wishing he would see me, wanting him to invite me to hang out. I desperately craved his friendship and respect. I was terrified that before we were able to build that as siblings, Mom's plan would cause an end game to the possibility.

I was not comfortable enough as a gay person to defend it to him. If he was disgusted or if he laughed at me or made fun of me, I would have been likely to believe him. I grew short of breath as my anxiety increased. I wasn't ready. I was pissed.

I sat on the couch where I'd been, and began to engage with a smirking, head-bobbing mother who said, "Where'd your friend go?"

"Mom, you're drunk."

"Yes, we had a nice time. We were celebrating your brother and I think it's time you tell him your secret."

"Mom, I'm not going to tell..." She interrupted me by slamming her palms down on the table between us, and spoke with alarming clarity, "Who the hell can I talk to about this?" She pushed herself up onto her knees and lunged toward my brother.

"Mom, not like this. I'm not ready, and he won't even remember."

"Joshua, wake up." She was bouncing the couch cushions beneath him now.

"Mom! Come on!"

"Jossshhhua! God damnit! Wake up!"

"Whaaaaaaaat!?" He mumbled with his eyes closed. She looked at me and smiled, then said, "Go. Tell him. Josshhua, your sister..."

"Mom, if you want him to know so badly, *you* tell him!"

"I promised I wouldn't tell anyone, so you have to."

"Mom! Not like this."

"Jenny, I gave you my word, so you have to."

"MOM!"

I got up from the couch and went into the pantry, to see if there were any bottles. If this was going to happen, I needed a drink. I found vodka to embalm myself with and took four gulps until I could breathe again.

I returned to the couch and lit a cigarette. "Oooh! Light me one, too." Mom reached over.

"Josh!" I resentfully barked. I eyed my mother through a call-your-bluff-exhale of smoke. "Wake up!"

He jumped and turned his startled and irritated eye slits toward me. "Huhhh!?"

"Mom wants to tell you something. Mom, I give you permission to tell him my secret since it's so important to you."

She nodded her head toward me while she pulled on her cigarette, accepting authority to disclose. As she exhaled smoke, she began speaking. Her words were slow coming. She wouldn't just rip the Band-Aid off, so to speak, like I wished she would. She was floating in a completely different level of drunk, where time bent differently than it did in my anxiety. It felt like the seconds beating a huge drum in exaggerated delivery of time.

"Joshua, you know how...well." Mom took a long drag of her cigarette and exhaled even longer than before. "You know how *you* like girls, Joshua?"

Mom began to cry, also in slow motion. The sniffles came first, pauses between words and drags of nicotine becoming more labored and distant from one another as she put the wrist of her cigarette-holding-hand to her lips in shame. Shaking her head and bobbing I watched as the dam broke—heaves of buried emotion ran her over like a train, with scattered moments of pulling herself back together. I pitied her for what my secret had done to her. She had held it to herself for two years, and I was oblivious to how hard it had been for her. Living in the undertow of my own fear, I'd failed to see her drowning in broken dreams for her daughter. I felt sad, until she'd try again.

"Joshua, you like girls different than you like boys. The way that you like girls, you know what I mean?"

Josh was fading in and out. "Mom, what?"

I sat watching this; imagining that all protection would be gone. Any hope that I had of my brother taking up for me was about to vanish. If he disowned me, if he said ugly things to me, I would just die. God, please hurry this up. God, please hurry this up. I began to wonder how much vodka was left in the kitchen. I lit another cigarette.

"*Mom.*"

"Well," her head extended to one side, preparing to let it all go. Her tongue clucked, and she raised the cigarette above her mouth to punctuate the air, her face draped with the expression of a flabbergasted woman who had an unfortunate detail to share with the other ladies in the sewing circle. "Well" her voice dropped to a whisper, "Jenny likes girls that way, too."

"Yeah? So?" Josh responded quickly and passed out again. I was vibrating with anger, with shame. I needed more alcohol.

"Are you happy?!" I barked at her.

Mom had fallen back on her heels and she looked at me, mascara smeared beneath her eyes. The beautiful woman I'd watched put on make-up when I was a little girl. What had I done to her? She shook her head from side to side slowly, forgetting she held a lit cigarette.

"Mom." Shame was smoldering in my gut. I looked at this woman and remembered dancing with her and singing into brushes.

"No, Jenny, I'm not happy." She paused and looked at me, and tears betrayed her. She shrugged her shoulders. "I'm not happy."

It was as if she was discovering this for the first time right in front of me. I watched her cry and suddenly I saw her—I saw the weight on her shoulders, the burden, the exhaustion. She stood up and pulled herself together, wiping her face. She sniffed and finally said, "No, I'm not, honey. I haven't been happy for a very long time."

Near silence held us up. Josh's snoring was the only sound. I felt so sorry that I couldn't be normal. I imagined how normal it might have been, if she had come home after drinking with Josh and I were someone else. Maybe my boyfriend and I would have listened to funny stories from their evening out and had a drink with them. So normal. But I'm not normal. I'm too much.

Mom said one more thing that night. "It's not your fault."

* * *

I woke the next morning terrified to address the day before. I didn't know if either Mom or Josh would remember. It wasn't uncommon for me to tell my mother the story of what she had done in a blackout. She swore she didn't remember things that I felt it would be impossible to forget, but she was determined. What could I do but take her word for it? I didn't know what I'd find, so I prepared for the worst.

I paused at the top of the staircase, to embolden myself for whatever conversation I might be confronted with. The house seemed quiet and calm. Three steps down, I could see out the window. Josh was in the back yard, hand-washing his new car. He appeared to be alone, so I wondered where my mother was. I descended the stairs and tiptoed around the house. She might still be sleeping. I decided to go outside and see what had happened.

The sidewalk from the house and through the yard to the gravel parking spot where my brother stood seemed miles long. I finally arrived and just stood there, allowing myself to be seen, giving him the chance to speak first, because I didn't know what to say.

He continued to wash his car without acknowledging me. This was not abnormal. Josh had found ways to survive our childhood, too. He'd gone largely inside of himself— deeply, safely inside where he could keep his anger from flying out of him. Most of the time he held it together with strength and silence. Josh is handsome and charming and hard working. He was sensitive, too. Not effeminate, but sensitive. I always thought he felt as much as I did, but since he was brought up in a body that was male, he had little or no freedom to speak of it.

I learned by watching my big brother. He'd protect his anger and let it out in small, inconsequential or useful bursts as he deemed appropriate. I wanted to be like him and wanted him to like me. I'd have given anything for Josh to like me. He was a star football and baseball player in high school. He'd been on Homecoming Court. Girls loved him, and all of his friends were in the popular crowd. I rarely knew if my girlfriends came over to see me or only to be near Josh.

He'd taken to turntables, and would lose himself for hours in headphones, mixing music. I suppose Josh tamed his insides with song. Frequently he'd play Genesis, and Phil Collins would scream, "See the lonely man there on the corner, what he's waiting for, I don't know...when he shouts nobody listens, where he leads no one will go—oh." Another song he'd mix into hip hop or would play repeatedly was by The Who. "No one knows what it's like to be the bad man to be the sad man behind blue eyes...no one bites back as hard on their anger, none of my pain and woe can show through...But my dreams, they aren't as empty, as my conscience seems to be..." I hoped and prayed that small pieces of Josh's hurt rode out of him on those lyrics—returning some semblance of balance to the pressure he carried inside.

My brother was good looking, quiet, and mysterious. Until he wasn't. When he sprung a leak, I wanted to run in and tackle him, holding my hands over the dam that had broken. His anger was terrifying. I wasn't afraid of him, because I knew we were on the same team. He didn't scare me because I knew he was good. But it pained me to watch him believe he had to carry it all. It was excruciating, not knowing how to engage with this guy I wanted to set free from his frustration, an anguish he'd never admit to carrying inside.

I couldn't tackle him. I couldn't repair the dam, and I failed every time I tried to get Josh to talk about his feelings. I had learned there is some relief in admitting the truth outside of myself. Granted, I mostly used my journal and art, but I released things instead of bottling it all up and felt a little better each time. Except about this. Being drawn to girls was something I had never spoken about to anyone, except Mom, until now.

I couldn't speak its name outside of myself. Not yet. So, I stood there as Josh washed his car to music, wondering if he'd acknowledge me, or if all of his energy was holding him together inside. He finally stopped and looked up quickly. "Hey," he said.

My heart leapt with hope. Either he remembered and it was okay, or he didn't remember and I was safe, for now.

"Hey. Whatcha doin?" I realized it was a stupid question. He didn't respond. I took a deep breath and prayed for strength. "Josh, do you remember talking with me when you got home yesterday?"

"Yeah."

"Do you remember what Mom told you?"

"Yep." He never appeared distracted from the car. A few moments passed.

"Do you have any questions?"

"Nope."

"We good?"

"Yeah."

"I love you, Josh."

"Yep. You, too."

I wanted to make the car vanish and run into his arms. I wanted him to hold me and tell me he understood how confusing all this was, and he didn't know the answers either, but he loved me and nothing would change that, and if I ever needed anything at all I could come to him and...But I knew better.

Much of what I needed was likely in that final, "You, too," and to push it could turn the tide dramatically. So I walked delicately in his silence and returned to the house, unsure of what was next, but sure that my brother knew I was gay and needed to deal with it like he tried to deal with everything else—quietly and alone.

CHAPTER SIX

My experience of a first girlfriend turned everything I knew on its head. I was fourteen, Zanni was seventeen. I wrote about our first kiss in my journal, which she frequently read, and she made me destroy it. I'd beg her to run away with me. I'd beg her to tell the world that she loved me. She'd tell me she would, then we had to stop this. Repeat. We will, we can't, goodbye. We will, we can't, goodbye.

I was learning, again, not to believe my experience, which had me convinced that our alone-time moments were true. I was good at seeking refuge between the lines in a fantasy of what few words people actually said to me. I had learned to ignore what I needed to spend my entire life peddling my dream to her. I was chasing the "I love you, baby." I held on through the boyfriends and her family's spoken and unspoken judgment. I held on through the self-deprecation it took to love her the way I did and pretend I hardly knew her in public.

I learned that boys provided adequate attention when she was in her "we can't" phase. Being touched and desired took precedence; I'd take acknowledgment from anyone willing to give it. I laid down with too many bodies to avoid being alone. I looked into far too many eyes that had just met me, hoping to believe what they believed they'd found in me.

The agony of young desire drew me to Zanni like bees to nectar. Except when I arrived at the source of my longing, her willingness to acknowledge me was unpredictable at best. Her boyfriend might be there, at which point I'd need to shut down and act like the dumb little friend she endured visits from. Sometimes I would arrive, and she would glaze over with joy to see me, sneak me up to her room, pull me into her arms and squeeze me to her, taking a deep breath from the crevice of my neck to devour my scent. She'd whisper, in a voice ragged from Marlboros, "Oh my God I missed you so much, baby. I need you." Those. Moments. Stood. Still.

Other times, she'd invite me over and when I arrived, she simply wouldn't be home, and I wouldn't hear from her for days. Later she would explain that something had come up and she didn't expect me to wait around for her. "What am I supposed to do?" she'd scream, "if my boyfriend comes by and wants to take me out? Should I have said no because I had plans with *you*? Yeah, that's not gonna happen." I felt that was a perfectly reasonable option—and also the truth—but her tone shamed me for thinking I deserved to be considered important.

I was so enamored with Zanni that I would beg her to be with me, despite her ongoing declarations of, 'I love you, come here, go away.' I didn't stand a chance to develop any self-esteem.

We were in high school. I had no idea what we were doing, or why I abandoned a sweet and loving boy like Javier to do it. Nothing made sense. I was obsessed. I wasn't even sure that gay was a legitimate thing.

The world had already shown me it didn't know what the hell it was doing, so if her argument was only, "We can't!" My question was consistently, "Says *who*?" Ministers? Moms? Dads? God? Those who profess marriage is sacred and kind? All bullshit. I was willing to trust myself on this one point to a degree that I'd never put confidence in myself before. I was certain of my love for her. I was certain of our capacity to care for each other in this troubled world. I was sure that her arms, her scent, were enough.

I was fourteen and I'd have gone on National TV to declare it, but Zanni wasn't having it. Not consistently. She'd beg me to not say anything to anyone because she wasn't ready, and it would hurt her. Sure, she'd humor me for an hour as we smoked cigarettes after sex. She'd dream with me and we'd laugh and pretend all would be fine somewhere far away. But then her boyfriend would come over and she'd act like she didn't know me. In hindsight, it's like I was jumping up and down, laughing and crying, desperately trying to grab the golden ring.

I imagined Zanni was the solution to all my problems. I could feel the collapse of every wall I ever built inside. Fantasy dictated that I would finally be free with her. Everything felt aligned when things were good with us, and yet it was a troubled situation. She had her own history of family dysfunction that affected her. She had her own shame that kept her from believing love might be good. I spent years trying to get her to attempt a monogamous partnership with me, but I never got her to seal the deal. I was not enough.

I leached what little life I could from the broken 'others' who sought me out. You find me attractive? You like this? Let's dance, I'll show you how sexy I can be. Look at this move I know, look at this sexy face I can make. Watch me throw my head back and laugh like a girl. I got it all, sweetheart, what do you want? Oh, you want to cum? I can do that, too. I realize now that approval was my first addiction. Unfortunately for myself and many other girls on this planet, figuring out who we are can be a long and exhausting process.

* * *

Playing sports helped me burn some of the confused energy that I contained most of the time. I had a lot of friends on my basketball team and I loved the bus rides home from away games. The bus was quiet, and I'd lean my head against the window, trying to make out mysterious forms in the darkness as we drove back to school. The farther the away game the better, because it afforded me more time to spend alone. I'd found Melissa Etheridge's music, and while she wasn't popular among the kids I hung out with, she understood me. Long before I'd find rooms full of other gay people to be around, I found her music. She'd sing to me through my Walkman and I could walk into her songs for refuge. Her voice was deep and sexy, and her lyrics acknowledged all of my secret feelings.

* * *

By my junior year, Zanni had begun a life free of the social pressures in high school. She'd found a lesbian bar full of women her age—yet another impossible hurdle between us that I refused to acknowledge. I kept myself in a tortured state by choosing to believe what I wanted. If I knew then what I know now, I might have taken her at face value and let her go.

She said it many times, that she was no good for me and she'd only hold me back; but I believed I could save us, that I could manage it, change her, fix it...I had no sense of what healthy relationships looked like, nor that I was deserving of one. I felt an emotional charge in the chaos, even in not having my needs met. I mistook this challenge for love. So, I persisted on the elusive chase, championed by a tragic misinterpretation of, 'nothing is perfect' and 'relationships are hard work'.

The bar she'd found was called Temptations, and it was pretty close to where I lived. I became curious. She'd tell me tales of this place and how it was full of people like us and it was amazing, and she loved being there and it was a different world. She said she felt normal for the first time in her life. Since she had found this new and exciting world, the possibilities were endless for her and now we really had to stop talking, because she and I could never be together again. It was great while it lasted, but she told me I had to let go. I wouldn't hear of it. Granted, I was only seventeen and I looked younger. I needed to find a way to be a part of that new world—her world. I couldn't imagine waiting three years to go to Temptations.

When I told Zanni to introduce me to her friends as her girlfriend, she wasn't about to tell them she was involved with a *kid* who was still in high school. She was adamant that I didn't belong in a bar because I could get in legal trouble for being under age. She made me promise because, she'd say, "I worry about you, babe, and you're too young for this world. I don't want it to ruin you."

Initially I agreed because I was putty in her hands, but eventually I learned that she'd been going with another lesbian couple we knew, both girls only a year older than I was! I wanted to die. How come she wouldn't take me?

* * *

I got off work at 10:00 p.m. and pulled the handwritten address out of my pocket. I was going to go and see what this place was like. It was the scariest and most exciting thing I'd ever done—second only to the first time we kissed. I lit a cigarette and started the car. I needed to see the place that was wedged between us. I needed to know the enemy, look into the face of my competition. I had to see for myself.

I drove past the entrance several times before I went in. It shared a parking lot with Jewel-Osco. There it sat, right in the open for everyone to see. I parked closer to the bar than the grocery store, so I could get a good look. My heart was racing; I was afraid I was going to get caught. Caught at what I wasn't sure, but I was scared to be there. I felt like an alarm might sound, alerting decent families who were going to the grocery store that I was dirty and perverted. The morality police might come and arrest me for having unnatural desires, or I'd see someone I knew and have to explain myself. I worried that I could get in trouble for being underage and in the parking lot of a bar.

Was it creepy to sit in my car without going in? Was I invading people's privacy by watching from inside my own fear? I was both ashamed and electrified at how badly I wanted to enter. I had to know if it was a place for me.

I was compelled to discover if I might fit in somewhere after all.

Women exited the cars around me, holding hands in the parking lot and walking toward the neon lights that spelled Temptations. I couldn't believe a place like that wasn't hidden away in some dingy corner of the town. I noticed that some of the women looked like men, and some like ladies. I'd never seen anything like it. In that moment, in that place, it looked normal. Couple-stuff was happening, a smack on the butt followed by playful laughter and a quick kiss. IN PUBLIC!? I was riveted by the possibilities, imagining Zanni and I getting out of the car one day... "Do you have my lighter? Wait, I think it's in the glove box. Hold on."

One day we could be doing basic people stuff, out in public. Together. They were all lesbians like me. Where were the scary gay people I'd heard about?

I sat in awe for an hour, chain smoking cigarettes. The tape I was listening to had ended, and I could hear muffled voices and movement outside my car. Everything from cowboy boots to leather vests to floor-length dresses paraded by. Then doors would slam, and more people would courageously disappear into a secret world that was alive with pulsating bass. Every time the bar door swung shut again, I felt it laugh at me—as if to confirm that she was right. I was just some dumb kid who didn't get to go in.

* * *

One day soon after Zanni had been going to the gay bars without me, she called and told me point blank on the phone that she was getting married. It was completely out of the blue. She said she thought I should know, and she would be leaving town soon and I'd never see her again. She also said that she wasn't gay, and she was going to marry a man. She barked that it was for the best and hung up before I could respond.

There was so much hurt in her voice, the kind she tried to camouflage with false confidence, but I could hear through it. What sounded like certainty to others screamed hopelessness to me.

Thomas was tall, fair skin, muscular, and Christian. He wasn't particularly attractive in my opinion, but he didn't need to be. He had the church and 'what is right and just and good' on his side. It was an arm wrestle I'd never win. I'd been defeated. I was not threatened by other women in her life, but that man with the muscles, the penis and Jesus, he represented things I could not compete with. If she wanted those things, she wouldn't find them with me. One moment she told me I was skinny with chicken legs, and the next she said I was the most beautiful thing she'd ever seen. She always assured me the boys were a cover.

I knew Thomas had been interested in Zanni for a while. He'd heard rumors about her and I being involved in secret, because his sister was on our basketball team. Guys didn't respect the idea of two girls having a relationship. Maybe two girls said they loved each other, and they were hugging and giggling together all the time, but girls were still made for boys. Nobody in the Midwest was raised to think of it as a real option that girls could want each other the way a boy wants a girl.

Here was my dilemma. I was in love with someone and nobody knew. You can't exactly defend a relationship that nobody knows exists.

I had to stand there and allow it when he'd step right between us and tell her how beautiful she looked. He'd offer to get her a drink, ask her to dinner. He'd take my place on the couch next to her, in the car next to her, and in the bed next to her. I couldn't say a thing. Now she wanted to marry him? It was against the law for me to marry her, so I could never offer her the security he could.

I was numb, and the receiver fell to the floor. This was worse than when my brother and his friend had come into my room and found me spooning her.

It was worse than when I had to sit in the back seat of another boyfriend's car and watch him pet her hair while she lay her head in his lap.

This was even worse than her mother catching us kissing in her bedroom. Her mother's cold disgust had lacerated our connection from the hallway. I was forced to walk past her entire family to exit the house in shame. Zanni didn't walk with me. She didn't protect me. She just whispered to me, "GO! GET OUT OF HERE!" I was powerless.

I rode my bike home crying and screaming at the top of my lungs, weaving in and out of parked cars recklessly. I threw my bike in the bushes and leapt up the steps into the house. I ran past everyone and up the stairs, three at a time, slamming the door to my room, locking myself into a space where the world would leave me alone.

It seemed I was always burdened with shame about things I couldn't control. I couldn't un-love her. I couldn't be a boy to make our love right, and I couldn't make myself older. I was coming up short in every way and operating from a deficit became my normal. Powerless, again. I couldn't be what I wasn't, but I just knew I could win her back if I got her alone, away from the world telling her our love was wrong. I planned to remind her of how much she loved me, until her boyfriend brought Jesus into it.

My mother called me to the front door, probably happy there was a man asking for me. I arrived and immediately worried that something had happened to Zanni. Why else would Thomas come to see me? Was she with him? Did she send him over to get her things? What was happening?

He asked if I'd come outside so we could talk. Concerned, I complied and came out to the porch. I sat on the top step and he sat on a step near the bottom, looking up at me.

"Suzanne said she told you she wants to marry me," he said with a smile, "so you know I'm going to make her my wife."

Heat shot from my toes to my temples. I wanted to kick him in the teeth. I was overcome with fantasies that left him decapitated or crying at the altar after I rescued her on their wedding day, and she ran away with me. I would not give him the satisfaction of falling apart.

"Yes, she told me. Congratulations."

You fucking fuckface mutherfucker, what gives you the right to sit on my porch? Somehow you feel entitled to visit my fucking house? I swallowed my rage because in truth, I had no power there either, not even in my own home.

"Thank you, we're very excited. I wanted to come and talk with you, to be sure you're okay and that we have your blessing."

"I don't understand."

"Well, I know that you and my fiancé, well, she says that you're in love with her and the news was hard on you, because she doesn't feel the same way. I like you, and I know that she's easy to love. So, I just want your blessing."

I thought I might throw up. Really.

"If you love her the way she says you do, I'm sure you want what's best for her. I know that your dad is a minister, so even though you choose to do something that God calls perverted, you wouldn't want to take someone you love into that decision. I'm a Christian man. Where I can take her is holy and right. That's what you want for her, isn't it?"

I felt like there was a skyscraper sitting on my chest. I couldn't speak. I just stared at his knowing smirk and said nothing. "It's brave that you're letting go of her so that she can live right with me. With Jesus. She's been through enough. I can take care of her."

I'd become so practiced with detachment that I couldn't feel anything anymore. My mind was racing, and my tongue had fallen dumb. Had she portrayed that I was some confused lesbian kid who was in love with her? Did she elude that she couldn't make me go away? The possibility raped me of any hope or esteem I'd collected over time; and he was still smiling. It was so easy for him—to come over saying he'd take good care of the most important person in my life. He came to secure my surrender—he wanted a verbal contract that I would vanish and let him have her.

He said that I was demonstrating selfless love by 'giving her to him and promising to never contact her again'. He encouraged me to move on, saying that if I prayed really hard, I could abandon my unnatural lust and find a good man to marry, too. That, he said, was what he hoped for me. It was none of his business, he admitted, what I chose to do with my life once he left this conversation; so long as I promised to leave his fiancé alone. He was, however, concerned about my safety going into community college. He said if I chose being a gay instead of a Christian, he would be willing, as payback for abandoning his future wife, to show up as a bodyguard-like presence on campus until people learned that I was 'connected to protection' and no longer harassed me. He laid out this offer casually and kindly, as if to say, "would you like some peas?"

I wondered if she knew he was at my house. He wanted me to abandon her in exchange for protection from homophobic college peers? He was offering insurance? He wanted to keep eyes on me, and suddenly, I saw a chink in his armor. I smelled blood.

Thomas knew that what Zanni and I had was real. He knew that if she went through with this, he was the consolation prize. Why was that okay with him? I felt powerful for a few seconds while pitying that he would marry a girl he knew didn't love him. I could see that he felt so powerless, he had come by to erase me from the story. I realized that she hadn't sent him. His visiting me was the only way he stood a chance with her and he knew it. And still, I lived in a world where he held all the winning cards.

* * *

By the time I graduated high school, I had a small group of friends I'd grown pretty close to. I've always felt lucky for that. I wasn't out to any of them when we graduated, but we were as close as a group of friends could be, minus that one small detail. We all got a hotel room and with the assistance of a helpful sister-in-law, managed to fill our luggage with alcohol and cigarettes for all of us to go party in downtown Chicago, to celebrate graduating.

My friend Aurora, or Rory, and I had something critical in common. She loved Melissa Etheridge. She loved her because she loved rock n' roll, and she was comfortable with admitting that she found her kind of sexy. I loved Melissa Etheridge because her tapes had provided solace for this young, closeted lesbian. I didn't tell Rory my reasons, I just told her that I liked Melissa, too. When we found out that she was going to be at the Arie Crown Theater, we bought tickets right away. Rory suggested that we go the night before and try to meet her by her bus. I doubted that things like that happened in real life, because it sounded like a movie. But I was game.

So, on July eighteenth, Rory and I drove out to McCormick Place and somehow made our way into the back area where we found Melissa Etheridge's buses. Rory knocked on the door and looked back at me with excitement. Eeeeek! To make a long story short, we met the bus driver and her whole road team. We flirted, hung out, and went back to the hotel bar, where they said Melissa might come down for a drink after her show. She didn't, but they did. They were good guys, but we were clear about our mission. When it became apparent that she wouldn't be joining us, we said thank you and decided to take off. We had tickets for the show the next night, and as if to apologize that she hadn't shown, the guys said they would get us hooked up the following night. They said we should meet them in front of the bus when we arrived the next day.

After an excruciating twenty-four hours, we did join them by the bus, and they had backstage passes for us. Suddenly the concert seemed secondary—my patience was truly exercised that night. Rory and I enjoyed the powerhouse rock n' roll show before we were led through tunnels and doorways to a small room. Her hair was wet from the shower and she'd taken off all of her rock n' roll attire. She stood below my eye line in jeans and a yellow and white chequered, short sleeve, collared shirt. I couldn't believe how small she was, that someone so tiny could have such an impact on my life, how someone so normal-looking had created the songs that had kept me hopeful enough to maintain a double life. I stood next to her, realizing that I looked like any of the million faces she saw on tour every week, faces that pulled her aside to take pictures.

I pulled out the letter I'd written to her. Rory didn't know I had it. I was going to hand it to Melissa and tell her to please read it another time. In the letter I told her what her songs meant to me. I told her that I was a lesbian, but still in the closet. I told her that the girl with me didn't even know I was gay, but I wanted her to know. I thanked her for being 'out'.

Melissa met my eyes briefly when she took the letter from my hand. She smiled before she placed it in her back-right pocket, holding the smile while she smacked her butt where she'd tucked it away. In that moment, being gay was larger than me. It was as loud as a rock concert and as real as she was standing there. A letter I'd written in private to the woman who'd sung to me in a Walkman Oasis for years, was now in her back pocket. I'd finally connected this thing inside of me with the outside world, beyond the bubble I was familiar with. I was reaching for a lifeline from a place of silence and shame, and she had received it, and smacked her butt to confirm it for me.

CHAPTER SEVEN

I didn't want to go to college. I could appreciate that others might, but for me, as soon as I was done with high school, I had every intention of moving to Chicago, studying improv comedy at The Second City where all the greats started, and then following the natural trajectory of my destiny to *Saturday Night Live*. I knew I needed to go right away and didn't care if anyone disagreed.

As it turned out, every adult in my life did disagree. They all felt it critical that I pursue college, and at eighteen I had so little fight left in me that I went. I applied to only one school, to appease the parental figures. I applied to my father's alma mater. If I couldn't do what I wanted to do with my life, then in the very least maybe I could create some sort of bond with my dad and he'd be proud of me.

On the other hand, if I wasn't accepted, no one could blame me because I tried, and I would have the rejection letter to prove it. Then I could go off to Chicago as planned and I would have done all that was in my power to please them.

I was accepted to Northern Illinois University, but none of the adults who expected me to thwart my dreams and go to college intended to pay for it. I had no knowledge of how money and interest worked in the student loan system. My uncle tried to show me, but my brain was on other things. I borrowed far more money than I needed and spent it all. I also worked during college and drank more than I went to class. I had no idea at the time that I'd be paying those loans back for the next twenty-two years, but I digress.

* * *

I headed to college convinced that if I was going to succeed, I needed to be a loner; stick my face in my studies and get it over with as soon as possible. That was the idea. I believed that there was a faraway place and time where I would eventually be who I was meant to be—

as soon as I could get out of here. Going to college was my first real escape from the circumstances I'd grown up in. I was sure that I could make college a new start and finally figure out who I wanted to be. What I didn't know was that how we grow up takes deep root in our adult behavior, and I'd developed patterns that would not be easily broken. Pleasing others, not advocating for myself, denying my heart's desires, and experiencing shame for loving differently were the masks and concessions I had relied on for years. Different faces played the current roles, but I reconstructed the façade I wanted to maintain among friends in college. My world was ripe with secrets and shame, stories meant for different people at different times. Much of what I did or didn't do lent itself to staying safe and not wanting to hurt people's feelings or make others uncomfortable.

I arrived at the dorm room I was assigned to as a freshman. Every door in the long triangle-shape hallway had two names on it; mine had only one. I took a deep breath laced with a glimmer of hope. Was it possible that I would have my own room and would not need to live in such close quarters?

I inserted the key and opened the door. The room was a small shoebox shaped space divided by an imaginary line down the center, simple and symmetrical. Two desks, two bolsters, two pull-out cots, two closets. Directly in front of me stood a heater beneath a tall window with drawn curtains. I could see well across the foggy campus through the glass. The claustrophobia I'd projected onto the next four years of my life began to dissipate. I could breathe. Suddenly I was hopeful that I might have this whole space as refuge from a closeted campus life. I could do that.

I went inside and set down the paperwork I'd gathered through orientations, lectures, and campus tours. Within this barrage of information was everything I needed to navigate campus to my classes, the student union, dining hall, gym, and library. In meticulous detail I was told phone numbers to reach places I didn't understand the purpose for yet, like *The Northern Star* and the *LGB Coalition*. Overwhelmed, I pulled out a creaky cot and contemplated my next move.

After several minutes staring out the window, I was taken by a desire to secure my single room. I couldn't realistically settle in until I knew whether I had a safe place or needed to get to know a roommate and navigate that relationship from the closet. The single dorm thing felt too good to be true.

I picked up a packet to start trying phone numbers and seek clarification. I called student services from the rotary phone on the wall in one of the closets.

"Hi, my name is Jen. I just got here today. I'm a freshman."

"Welcome, Jen! How exciting!"

"Yeah, thanks. Well, I thought I had a roommate but when I got here there is only my name on the door, so it looks like I have my own room, which is fantastic, but before I get too attached to the idea, I want to be sure it isn't a mistake."

"Well, Jen, I'm glad you called. I'll have to look you up and see what happened. Typically, if you didn't pay for a single room you'll have a roommate. Did you pay for a single room?"

"I don't know. I don't think so. I was sure I'd have a roommate, so I probably didn't. I think I would have known."

"Fair enough. Let me see, yes. Here you are. You are in the Towers, right?"

"The Towers?"

"Yes, I'm sorry. The building you're in, it's tall like a high rise, right? There are a few of them, we call them 'the Towers'."

"Oh, yes, that's right. God I'm such a freshman."

"Well, it's where everyone starts, Jen, so no worries. I'm reading here, and it says that the roommate you were originally assigned is no longer coming to school here, so for now you'll be alone. That said, if you didn't pay for a single room, you'll be assigned someone eventually. At least you get first dibs on which side you like while it gets figured out!" Her enthusiasm eluded me. "Do you have any other questions?"

"Yes, I do. Is it too late to pay for a single room? How much does it cost?"

"Well, it's not too late, but it will cost an extra $500 to keep the dorm as a single."

"Oh."

"Is that something you can do?"

"I don't know. I'm here completely on financial aid. So, is that something I can do?"

When I was growing up, there wasn't extra money. Rarely if ever. To this day, when money issues come up, I recoil into defeat. As soon as I learned that it would 'cost more', I expected it to be out of my league. Typically, I would resign my efforts and surrender to the reality that I couldn't afford it. The good ol' 'what's the use of trying' would kidnap me and I'd move on, often feeling sorry for myself.

In this situation, however, I had a stronger resolve. I was in a place where I would get lost walking out the front door. I knew no one, was surrounded by girls and guys I'd never met on a co-ed floor, and I was terrified of being in the closet. Having my own room would be a life saver. I was willing to do the thing that I hated doing most, the thing that makes me feel small and inadequate, the thing that shines attention on my mother as a 'can't provide in this way' parent. I was going to ask my dad.

Dad had long been remarried and was living in Wisconsin. His life was separate from mine in many ways, except when money became a need. I knew it and it broke my heart because I wanted a relationship with him, but I also had a hard time swallowing his new life. I had a hard time with the memories of our broken family.

It felt like a house was sitting on my chest when I had to reach out to him. I wanted to be his little girl again, but he had a new one. I wanted to be in a fluid relationship with him, but pain had built a mote around normal conversation. I didn't know how to talk to him; I felt stupid and inadequate when I did. I needed him in ways I could feel deeply, but not articulate.

Dad's second daughter, Jeanne, was about seven years old at the time and in my heart, it felt like she had gotten my dad and my life. Dad had stopped drinking and done some healing of his own. When he met and married his second wife, I had seen that he was happy. I had seen a freedom in his spirit I wasn't familiar with. I was jealous. I was jealous of his new family.

Dad was still ministering; he loved and served Jesus Christ as he had my whole life. I felt like his world was cleaner, more organized, and more prosperous than the one I inhabited. I felt angry about being 'left behind'. I felt like I was intruding on his new family when I wanted to talk to him or be with him. I wanted him to be happy, so decided I should stay away. Besides, everyone told me I looked like my mother. Why would he want to see me if I reminded him of the woman he had divorced? When I did approach him, I wanted to appear together, smart, and independent. I wanted him to be proud of me, but I didn't want him to know that.

I failed miserably, repeatedly, because in my youth I had not yet mastered self-regulation. I often overreacted or underreacted, and the former can appear unstable while the latter presents as cold and apathetic—I've even had it described as arrogance.

I wanted to be okay with everything, finally. It had been nearly ten years since my parents' relationship dissolved. When was I going to be okay with this 'new' reality? I felt stuck in the past; concrete boots buried in wet sand that everyone else had somehow stepped around. I beat myself up. "Get over it already! What's wrong with you?"

I often wanted to disappear. Alcohol helped with that, but alcohol also solidified being stuck. I couldn't move forward. I wanted a relationship with my sister because I loved her so much, yet I was jealous of her relationship with Dad and didn't know how to behave. The space between her and I was already loaded. I was a stranger entering her world; I had to learn my father again and keep myself from speaking about our memories, lest I mention other people from our other life, not to be discussed here. The tension silenced me.

My sister didn't know he had taken his only daughter (at the time) to the state capitol on a small yellow school bus. I had gone on a date with my daddy in third grade because I won the Young Author's Contest. She didn't know that I still had the winning manuscript, the one where my mom drew the pictures and my dad typed the story I wrote. She didn't know I had him first and life was happy once, until it wasn't. I don't think my sister knew there was another version of our father that I had grown up with, how his pain had caused him to behave by the end of our family's story, how he had used alcohol, and how deeply that affected the first family he built.

I knew alcohol was a problem for me. I made a conscious and private effort to control when I drank and how I drank around others. My drinking problem was a second—albeit subconscious—reason for wanting to keep my freshman year dorm room a single. I needed two things: a place to be where I didn't have to play the pronoun game or pretend to be straight; and a place where I could drink enough to disappear from all the secrets I had accumulated.

"If you can come up with the extra money, we can designate your dorm room a single this semester. You have a little time to get this figured out and you'll remain a single in the meantime. Call me next week at this time and tell me what you want to do. Welcome to Northern Illinois University, Jennifer. Let us know if there is any other way we can help you."

"Thank you." I hung up the phone. I knew that the only person in my life who might have the extra money to help me keep this room as a single was my father. Since I hated asking him for things and I was sure that even if I did ask, he would refuse, things didn't look good. I decided to get some food before confirming whether this was important enough to humiliate myself.

"Hi, Dad. It's Jen."

"Jenny! How's college life?"

"So far so good, Dad. It's actually why I'm calling though."

"Oh yeah? Great, I'd love to hear how my alma mater is these days. What's up?"

"Well, actually, how are you doing?"

"Things around here are pretty normal. Leah is cooking an amazing dinner like she always does, taking good care of us. I just got out of the garden, my tomatoes are looking good this season. I wish you could see them for yourself. Hugh and Jeanne are keeping busy with their friends, Jeanne is practicing her piano lessons right now. We'd love to have you come visit, any time you like. Our home is always open; we'd love to get to know you and have you get to know us."

"Thanks, Dad, I know it is. Thank you."

I wanted a life that looked like what my father described as normal. I didn't feel like it was available to me. I was in deep conflict over his invitation, again, and resented that it seemed so easy for him to say what was painful for me to hear and decline. Again. I'd spent years wanting to take him up on this offer, but I didn't know how to get to his house. I had no car. I also didn't know how to be gay in a home filled with Jesus and Christianity and a seemingly perfect family. I didn't know how to not look dirty and dumb and messy in that setting. I didn't know how to spend time with my step-brother or sister and not envy their place in his family. I didn't know how to engage with his wife and not resent her for being able to make him happy. He extended the same invitation every time we talked, but I didn't know how.

I assumed I was really messed up because of all the barriers between Dad and me. I was abnormally cruel and sensitive. I felt so many different things—it had to be me. I knew that if I went there, I would feel like a five-year-old wanting to scream, "Look, Daddy! Look at me!" constantly wanting all of his attention, and that wasn't appropriate. I wanted to get to know my sister without seeing myself in her face and wishing she and I could switch places. I wished that she had my life and I had hers. I wanted to love her and not resent that when my parents divorced, I had to stop piano lessons and violin lessons because my mom couldn't afford it. Now she was using my piano lessons. She was playing songs that I'd never had enough lessons to master.

I had a lot of pain in the way of me loving the people I wanted desperately to be close to. I didn't know what to do with it. I hardly still had a relationship with God that I could draw strength from to do the hard things. I wanted to take Dad up on his invitations, but I was terrified of making the investment in learning to love them only for it to all be taken away again when they learned of me being gay. I couldn't stand the thought of it. Fear over my father withdrawing his love again, proving that I was not lovable on a whole new level, I couldn't bear it.

I was sad. I was angry. Hurt, vulnerable, and afraid. I couldn't experience losing my family again.

"Well, Jenny, I'm so happy when you call me. What's going on?" His voice glistened with joy and peace. I felt like I would start crying if I said another word. I put on my armor by deciding I didn't care how it went. The call was a means to an end. Stay on task, Jen.

"Well, I'm in my dorm..."

"You're in the Towers, right? I lived in a few places, but the closest I stayed to the Towers was Lincoln. Tell me about your roommate!"

"Well, that's why I'm calling, Dad. I don't have one. I called student services to see if it was a mistake, and I learned that the person I'd been paired with decided not to attend this semester. So, I'm sitting in my dorm room and it's small. I can't believe two people are expected to live here together! I asked the lady if I can just keep a single instead of being assigned a roommate, and she said I can keep the room as a single, but I have to pay more. I would really like to keep the room as a single, but I don't have $500."

"Why would you want a single room? No way. Get a roommate. Roommates are one of the best parts of the college experience. I think you'd be cheating yourself, Jenny. I think you should get a roommate."

I wanted to connect with the joy in his voice. I wanted to wrestle out of my fear and find him to be right. He was speaking from the context of his own college experience some thirty years earlier, on this very same campus, unpacking his things and meeting his roommate. He was new on campus back then just like I was now, and I wanted to be strong like he sounded. I cherish the things Dad and I have in common. They forge a common thread between us. I was forever trying to draw lines that proved he belonged to me.

I was not my father; I didn't want to meet my roommate. I didn't want to be there at all. I was gay and scared and controlled by alcohol, and everyone I'd ever wanted to be close to seemed to walk away. I didn't want to make friends, didn't want to experience college, and didn't want to tell him that my world was not his world. I wanted to drink and stop feeling; and stop wanting girls before he found out about it all. That's what I wanted.

The silent pause between us was approaching an uncomfortable stretch and I remembered it was my turn to talk. "I like my personal space, Dad. I'm going to meet a lot of people here. I mean, what if we have different study habits? We might not like the same music. I want to do well here. I really don't want to get stuck with some party animal that I have to work around."

I thought I had made an iron-clad case. "Anyway, I was hoping you could help me with the $500 to keep it a single. Will you help?" I felt my body slump as my request landed in silence. I prayed for mercy. I prayed for guilt to plague him into a yes—that usually worked with my mother. The problem was she never had extra money. I sat a rigid mess the .6 seconds that it took him to respond.

"Oh, no, I'm not going to buy you out of the experience of having a roommate. I think you'd be stealing from yourself. If you want a single room, you'll have to ask your mother or come up with it yourself. I don't think it would benefit you."

"Okay, Dad, well, I thought I'd ask. Thank you anyway." I needed to get off the phone immediately or he would hear me fall apart.

"I'll call again soon. I love you."

"Okay, goodbye, Jenny."

I was startled by the surge of rage that hurled the receiver against the wall across the room. "*Fuck!*" I yelled. Then it occurred to me that he might still be on the phone, so I quickly stood up to retrieve it and slammed it at least six times against the receiver before I wondered how thin the walls were. Heaving with emotion and staring out the window, a fresh claustrophobia set in as I felt new closet walls erecting slowly about my shaking body.

I was trapped and afraid. And suddenly thirsty.

Dr. Martin Luther King, Jr. told the truth that I was starving for. I was an actor living a double life and tried to protect my heart from feeling, but his sermons rocked my world. My spirit felt a kinship to his plea for equality. I appreciated how at twenty-five years old, he got thrown into the forefront of a movement.

My closeted connection to Dr. King's spirit allowed me a place to seek God and justice when I'd determined I was not worthy. I discovered his audiotape set, *A Knock at Midnight*. There I found some of the most powerful sermons I've ever heard that, sadly, are still relevant today. I was moved by his oratory, his insight, and his angry compassion. His offensive agape love in the face of expressed hatred.

The more I read and learned, the more I saw the reaction to King's message was a mixed bag. His words felt so true to me; I couldn't conceive of people's agitation with him. Their contempt frightened me because people can become violent. I suddenly wanted to become a minister like my father, stirring and puncturing public constructs the way Dr. King did, but doing it for the queer community. I dreamed of bringing the gay community back to God. I wanted to believe that God never rejected us, that people are the only ones who hold fear in their hearts.

I knew we were genuine, colorful, loving, and creative. I also knew that we were dying of shame, turning to drugs, alcohol, and sex instead of to God. I remember my father saying that he was afraid for me, choosing to be part of such a sick community. Yes, some of the gay community is promiscuous, and addicted, and more frequently suicidal than straights; but we aren't those things because we are gay. We are those things because we've been taught that God doesn't love us. Think about that for a moment. We were taught that God didn't love us.

We struggled to shed the parts of ourselves that were unacceptable, while becoming the things the world said we ought to be. Some church people shamed us; many families disowned us. We didn't feel welcome in the heterosexual world; the culture essentially left us out. Abandoned and alone.

I began to believe that if I had the nerve to say out loud what was true in my heart, I might find freedom. I knew it could be dangerous because when you challenge people's beliefs, particularly if they are aligned with their understanding of religion/faith, it can become volatile. I prayed directly to God for the courage to be true to myself and close to Him. I'd try to get back to God and please my dad by attending different churches around my college town. I'd go to places that seemed more diverse than the church I grew up in.

Repeatedly, my father would tell me these places were cults and if they were not Bible-teaching churches, they were dangerous. If I wanted to go to church and get the support of people who love God, then I had to do it from the closet and endure check-ins about boyfriends, marriage, and children. This was particularly painful because in the 90s, marriage was an option unavailable to queer people, unless one chose to concede the fight for love in exchange for a place to belong.

Gay people could follow the truth of their hearts into seclusion from family, friends, and society—or go with the flow of pleasing others to have a place in the (straight) world. This required spending a lifetime lying to loved ones, which begins to feel less like a lie and more like the truth as it grows rings of shame around one's soul, the way a tree shows its age.

When I learned of Malcolm X, I was again encouraged. His blatant exploration of beauty and power and value inherent in black folks inspired me; folks who were socially deemed second class—people filled with shame born of lies. I wondered if that could be true of me.

Could I, as a queer person, actually have beauty and power and inherent value to declare?

Malcolm X made people angry with his unflinching assertion of self-value in the face of a racist society. I believe he and Dr. King planted a seed in me. I believe that somehow, listening to those two black men—second class in our society's eyes—gave me hope. Maybe behind the issues they faced, maybe next in line to their plea for equality, maybe there was a place for me. I wasn't sure and it wasn't until college that I started to test my theory.

* * *

My little brother and I hung out when he returned from Dad's. We'd always been close, but we needed to get to know each other again. It was his freshman year homecoming at the high school I had just graduated from. There are five years between us. We were drinking at a friend's house across from the football field, and I asked him to come outside with me while I had a cigarette. I told him I needed to tell him something.

He followed me without question, as he often did. When we were younger, I read him to sleep many nights. I mothered him when Mom was working multiple jobs and came home late. Bo's opinion of me was very important, and I was terrified to tell him my truth, but the lying by omission and pretending I had been doing around him was taking up all of my energy. I couldn't do it anymore. I hated to have bullshit between us.

I lit a cigarette, we sat down, and I just spit it out. He studied my face closely and then asked simply, "Why? Why would you do that?" That threw me for a loop. He was dumbfounded. He had seen me date guys before, so to him it appeared that I had simply changed my mind. He went on to tell me that a lot of his friends thought I was cute, so why would I date girls? I could easily get a boyfriend!

I made an effort to explain that being gay was something I had discovered, rather than something I had chosen. I told him that the only decision was whether to live in a way that honored who I was and how I experienced love or live my life to appease the expectations of others who didn't know the real me.

Bo sat with that for a few minutes and became very quiet. Then he asked if he could tell me something, too. "Of course," I said. "Yes."

His eyes looked down and when they came back up to meet mine, they were full of tears. Having just told him the most horrible thing I thought a sibling could ever hear I couldn't imagine what he was crying for. "Bo?" His nose started to run, and he sniffed hard to keep the snot inside.

"Jenny, I don't want you to be mad at me." I stared into his face. My little brother. I've always loved his precious, round, rosy-cheeked punim. With tears in his eyes my heart easily broke.

"What, Bosse? What is it?" His crying intensified and his chest heaved. The words exploded from his fourteen-year-old-lips. "I smoke." He collapsed into his hands and I had to keep from relief-laughing.

My God! I thought he was going to say he had gotten someone pregnant or he hurt someone, or...I shuffled my butt toward him and put my arms around him. I hadn't expected this conversation to end in my comforting him.

"Are you really crying about this?" I rubbed his blond hair until he pushed my hand off his head and looked up. "Aren't you mad? I was so scared you would yell at me."

"Well, smoking is dumb. I wish I didn't do it and I wish you wouldn't do it, but I do. And I guess you do, too." I exhaled. "I crazy love you anyway." He sniffed again and looked at me, restored. He smiled a smirk of relief. "I'm so glad that's over."

"Hey, Bo?"

"Yeah?"

"You did hear what I told you, right?"

"Yeah, and you looked as scared to tell me as I was to tell you."

"So. I'm gay. You smoke. We're fucked. Anything else?"

We sat in silence for a few minutes, absorbing everything we'd learned.

"Hey, Jenny?"

"Yeah?" He sat there, looking down at the ground. What now, I wondered? "Can I bum a smoke?"

* * *

I was riding the bus to class and reading *The*

Northern Star, our college newspaper. I was feeling particularly alone that morning and skimmed over the student-illustrated comic strips. I was jarred by a grave deficiency in representation. In every comic strip there were white guys who were either partying, trying to pick up girls, or otherwise competing with each other about something—at least that's what I saw that day. I picked my head up to scan the other bussing students and I saw black and brown faces, male and female faces, young and old faces, and someone with a cane and a body brace.

I looked again at the comics and felt a strong urge to produce something that allowed more of us to see our likeness represented on the printed page. I missed my stop because I'd lost interest in class and was on fire with this new-found purpose. I wanted nothing more than to get back to the dorm and begin. I'd never done a comic strip before and didn't know what to write about, but I decided that the content would be secondary to the visual representation of diverse students. Whatever words or ideas the characters spoke, it would be girls and guys of different races and ages, sizes and shapes. I would show people themselves in the newspaper, so they could feel included and recognized in our college community. I see you, I thought. I see us, and we deserve to be in print too.

The editor of the newspaper was a skinny, thoughtful, awkward character with remarkable self-esteem and confidence in his own opinions. Markos and I spent hours discussing our desire to see the world fight in ways that mattered—fights that included things like consciousness—without war; without killing and oppressing the poor and the gay and the brown. We dreamt of a world that valued more than money and power, a world that paid people equally, honoring talent and possibility over circumstances of birth. I'd smoke entire packs of cigarettes and drink multiple pots of coffee with him. I appreciated having someone to discuss worldly matters with, who was capable of seeing both an intellectual aspect and one of love and justice. Markos understood politics and history in a way that I didn't, and we would vent our anger about the systemic denial of people's human rights in various socioeconomic tiers. Markos knew I was a lesbian and that there was talk brewing on campus about it. He also knew I preferred to let rumors swirl as I hid in the closet.

There was a time when I thought Markos made a young journalist's error of confirming my sexuality in print after I'd shared it 'off the record' over coffee, but in hindsight I doubt that his outing me was a naïve mistake. I was scared of saying I was gay out loud, but the consciousness heating up on campus in the age of "Don't Ask, Don't Tell" needed a confirmed leader. He saw strength in me that I didn't know I had. He'd found trouble in the military because of his gentle demeanor and the assumptions people made, even though he identified as straight. He sought individual freedoms that allowed autonomy in people's lives. I admired that.

Although my sexuality was a personal, private pain that colored my passion for social justice, I wouldn't have volunteered myself as homosexuality's advocate. It made me far too vulnerable. I was willing to align myself with the cause of racial justice because it felt safer than putting myself out there and reaping such personal attacks. Markos saw the growing potential to talk openly about sexuality. He recognized that we had this platform—I produced a comic strip that was stirring the pot, and he was the editor of the paper! I believe he already had a desire for the larger conversation he would begin with Daily Kos one day. A decade earlier, he wanted to open talks and generate more dialogue that could benefit our small college town.

Today I choose to tell the story this way. I don't expect that Markos' Student Opinion titled, "Racial Problems and the Double-edged PC Sword" was aimed to hurt me. His written word on that Monday in October, in fact, actively supported me and my personal plight as a lesbian. In hindsight, I believe he saw the impact we could have, and feeding his own desire to see people squirm while getting me moving, he used his column to all but blow my closet doors off the hinges. What he wrote left me utterly exposed, and I was forced to finally face myself. Like a friend at the edge of a pool tired of watching me dip my toe in cold water, Markos pushed me in. He outed me in a column without ever gaining my permission, and he apologized when reality hit me and drove me anxiously to his office to ask him, *why?*

The trajectory of my college years changed dramatically that day. I no longer had patience for my classes because suddenly real life was happening. As far as the campus and the small town I lived in were concerned, I was no longer a student. I was The Lesbian. I felt more alone and vulnerable than ever.

Things went rogue at the newspaper and I spent the next four years leading a movement in plain view of my small world while losing my shit in private. My drinking and relationships turned me inside out. This time was anything but graceful. Suffice it to say that if I'd spent my twenties growing up in the throes of the entertainment industry in Chicago, LA, or New York, rather than safely on a college campus—I doubt I'd be alive to tell this tale.

The year was 1994 and suddenly, I found myself thrust into the spotlight within The Northern Star. It wasn't long before you could open the newspaper every day of the week and read something about homosexuality in general or how the paper ought to fire the *fucking dyke*

Jen. As my name was becoming known, people began to find me. Most frequently I'd be approached by closeted gays terrified of being harassed, beaten, raped, killed, or disowned if they were found out. They would get notes to me in daylight, like kites in a correctional facility. They would communicate in ways that flew beneath the radar so as to not be detected by their peers. On more than five occasions these notes vaguely requested that I meet them somewhere on campus, after dark, because they needed to talk but were afraid to be associated with me and my "out status".

I was compelled to get more involved so that my activity would match the focus I was enduring in the paper. I signed on as co-president of the Lesbian Gay Bisexual Coalition (LGBC). Part of my job was outreach and education. Our membership was a very small but visible army of students and staff willing to be seen. We'd receive many requests for LGBC panel speakers, to visit classes around campus and provide students the unlikely experience of talking with a real, live gay person. What an education we could provide!

We were invited to speak to diversity policy panels at local banks, schools, and businesses. There were most often two of us responding to those requests. Miguel and I, co-presidents, fielded most of the calls ourselves. I told people I'd never met about things I'd never said out loud. I feigned comfort with myself that didn't exist because my role was critical in developing perceptions. Questions I was asked as a panelist would trigger me, and both my public and private drinking took on more serious proportions.

I'd also taken to the relief provided by marijuana. I began to smoke so much that I'd lose track of days. The increased drinking and smoking were coupled with the stress of representing the gay community well. I wasn't ready to be a mascot for a group of people I was still ashamed to belong to. I also was not willing to let homophobic people around town and campus get away with it. I have always had a heart for justice and kindness—but at the time it needed to float in liquor and false pride, or I might have imploded.

Hell, Ellen DeGeneres didn't come out on her TV show and then Oprah for another two and a half years. There really was no one to point to; I was it. I took it upon myself to answer every written Student or Community Opinion column. It became my personal mission to represent well in the pages of the newspaper because there were closeted gay people all over the place secretly stealing refuge in my responses to ignorance. I knew that people who would never show up to support me were counting on me to support us. I was a voice for many people who were too afraid to have one.

For a while it felt like I was the only gay person in the world. Life felt heavy, and liquor kept it balanced precariously on my shoulders. I spent so much of my time worrying about being attacked or hurt or killed because I was gay. I never knew who to trust and who to believe. By then I was a blackout drunk. I'd instruct friends not to have sex with me no matter what I said while drinking, because I was gay and didn't want to have sex with them. I delegated the responsibility of taking care of me to other people; it had become normal practice. I'd spend days reconstructing the timeline of an evening to learn that I had spent time alone in a locked room with a guy...I'd get angry when I asked him about it, and he would proudly report that he only let me blow him because he knew I was gay.

I was disgusted with how others treated me when I was drinking. I couldn't understand why they wouldn't just behave the way I asked them to behave. Every time I was sexual with a guy it confused me and others who knew. Every time I touched a penis, it chipped away at my personal integrity as a lesbian who deserved respect and equal rights. Consensual sex with men didn't make me sick like people told me it should because I was gay, but it also had nothing to do with my heart. The impact I had on guys had become a coping mechanism prior to my coming to terms with my sexual orientation. The world told me I was supposed to be with males, but that was merely a behavior for me. Meanwhile, the world dictated that my natural attraction to women was the behavior I needed to stifle, correct, and avert. In actuality, women are more grounded in spirit for me.

It would be years before I had the spiritual and self-confidence to recognize that the consensus of church folk and vocal hate groups was born of ignorance—a total misunderstanding of how sexual orientation defines itself. The world claimed that one way was natural, and one way was deviant. That may be true for the majority of people, but I am a minority. I had to learn what was inherently natural for me, and trust that I only needed to be right with God about it.

Fortunately, I never had my photo set alongside anything I wrote in the paper, and graciously this was in a world before iPhones and social media. Therefore, word of mouth was the main way that people found me. Just going to class could break my anonymity wide open. Once a teacher called role on the first day of class and I raised my hand, the room discovered and discussed me at once. It was a murmur I'd grow accustomed to, but it was unnerving, never knowing if I was safe.

CHAPTER EIGHT

I was haunted by the possibility that my father would get an alumni letter outlining the chaos brought on by a perverted lesbian student who shared his last name—an entire issue devoted to the sick twenty-something who was ruining life on campus at his old school, obviously yearning to be excommunicated from all things decent. I admit it was a bit of a grandiose and self-centered fear. Nonetheless, I had to get in front of the possibility. I had to be the one to tell him I am gay.

All I needed to do was come to terms with the fact that more likely than not, my news would be the guillotine to finally separate us permanently from each other's lives. It would be the news that would make my biggest fear come true, that I was not good.

I gave my father tremendous authority over my worth. The attention I wanted from him was tied to my permission to belong to God. I wanted more time to figure things out, to make sure I was really gay. What if I'm wrong? What if I'm just confused? What if I have misunderstood myself for the last ten years and telling Dad will be a mistake I can never recover from?

If my father had disowned me and forbid me to see my sister, that would have plummeted me. I clung desperately to the hope that one day we would get all of this straightened out (no pun intended). I was afraid that my news would shut the door to any possibility I held out for a better relationship with all of them one day.

I sat down to write a letter, but my pen was constipated. I couldn't believe in myself long enough to write a full sentence. I started and stopped that letter for weeks, filling my trash can with snowballs of one-line drafts. I prayed and drank and cried and worried between drafts. I would drink at night to stop hating myself, to stop listening to myself, to stop being myself.

One night in the dorms, lying not a foot and a half from my sleeping roommate, a 'friend' of ours stumbled drunk into our room. He'd 'fallen in love' with me, he'd professed for months and months, picking me up from classes, walking me to the bus, calling to talk, taking walks, hanging out whenever I was around. I had told him for months that I wasn't interested in him that way. He was one of those I'd mess around with in a blackout, then get upset about it afterward. That day I'd had enough, and I told him I was gay. He laughed it off but admitted that now things made more sense.

That night, he staggered in, drunk, and got in bed with me. I was almost asleep as he started kissing me. I hit him and told him to get off me. He chuckled and told me to take it easy. I lost mobility as his weight held my limbs down. I tried to knee him in the crotch but couldn't move. He had me pinned, so I bit his lip. '*Ouch!*' he flashed a drunk smile, and quickly packed himself into me.

I've been here before, I thought as he got off all over my stomach. He laid on top of me and his own mess, breathing heavily. He whispered onto my face with hot, sour alcohol breath that he knew I was gay, but it didn't matter, because he still loved me. I hit him with my fist on the head and he got up laughing in a whisper—stumbling in the dark to fasten his jeans. Choni was still asleep or had taken to faking it. I told him to get the fuck out through clenched teeth.

I found a towel in the dark and walked down the brightly lit dorm hallway to the shared bathroom to wash him off of me. I stood in the running water wanting to scream and punch walls and explode out of these layers of confusion—but I was silent. I didn't want to wake anyone, so I behaved. I washed the towel in the shower water and rung it out as much as I could. I wore it wet back to my room and made as little noise as possible changing into dry clothes and hanging the heavy towel on my desk chair. I got back into bed, but I never fell asleep.

The next day, our group, my roommate and our friends—including him—met in the dining hall for lunch like we always did. His breath was still sour but mixed with cologne now when he leaned over to me. "Hey, I probably shouldn't have come to your room, but I was drunk." That was his and my secret for a year as he became one of Choni's best friends, and I sat a silent partner in the deal. I was frequently drinking to blackout. My hangovers were intense. I used alcohol to feel better, but then it started causing problems and I'd drink less. When drinking less didn't make me feel better I'd increase it again and coupled my drinking with marijuana. That helped. The combination helped to hold me together as I fell apart for the next several years.

Once again, I sat down to write a letter to my father. I made a list of bullet points— the things I couldn't afford to leave out. I needed him to know that I loved God, that I loved him and his family, and to please not take them away. He needed to know that part of why I didn't try harder was because I didn't know where I fit anymore. I explained my experience and sealed the letter, addressed it, and put a stamp on it.

Before I went to sleep that night, I did what I'd done a hundred times before. I got scared and ripped up the letter. My roommate would ask how the letter was coming. She'd comfort my fears about Dad; asking me how long I would put myself through this. She encouraged my engagement in the community and the newspaper. She'd love me no matter what, she promised, and she did.

Drinking and smoking weed didn't only induce promiscuity; it also helped me deal with increasing anger. I was full of anger and self-pity. I hated anyone for saying I was beautiful, especially when they were on top of me. I was angry that I didn't feel safe in church, and I hated myself for not feeling worth the love I wanted and needed. I told myself I was too stupid to be in love with my high school boyfriend.

For a long time, sex was something I got myself drunk enough to endure or initiate. Sex was what I would revert to when my heart hurt too much to breathe, when I was too drunk to care, and when I'd lost the capacity to hold myself together. I'd fall carelessly and pitifully into any waiting arms, regardless of who they belonged to.

I wrote another letter to my father and this time I was certain I would mail it, because I had noticed that my drinking and behavior were deteriorating around the fear of what he would say. I needed to have it over with one way or the other. It hurt too much not to know. I asked Dad to please write me back. I told him I couldn't bear to talk to him on the phone, I would need to see his response in writing. I addressed it, stamped it, and left it by the door so I would remember to bring it to the mailbox. As I left for class, however, I decided I would mail it the next day.

That evening when I got back to my room, Choni was under a blanket on her bed, watching Jerry Springer. I sat down to take off my shoes when she said, "I went to the mailbox after class. I brought your mail down and sent it too."

My entire body went hot. She must be kidding!

"Choni, I left the letter to my dad by our door. Did you see it?"

"Yep. I mailed it." She looked at me and said, "I love you, and I can't watch you do this to yourself anymore. Whatever happens, we'll get through it."

* * *

We were getting ready to head out to dinner when the phone rang. Choni answered it in her bouncy, "Hey, it's Choni" tone, which went flat when she said the second line. "Sure. She's right here. Hold on." She held a hand over the talking piece and extended the phone to me with both hands. Her mouth made shapes that told me it was him. My stomach went sour and I pulled out my chair. My mouth watered, and I grabbed the phone. "Dad?"

I didn't say much during that phone call. Mostly I listened, because the quality of my dad's voice told me it was a very difficult call for him to make, and once he started talking, I didn't want to miss a word. He told me he was surprised by my recent letter and grateful that I love him and Leah enough to want to share this part of my life with them. He said he didn't understand, and he was sure this would make my life very difficult, but he doesn't love me any less than he did before I shared this with him. He said that his wife Leah always thought I was gay—she even said so to him when I was about thirteen. Leah knew there was something different about me. Dad said the lifestyle I was choosing was not one that he believed in and was one that his faith did not embrace. He told me he didn't understand why I would choose this. He also said that we were both adults and could make our own decisions about what we do, believe, and how we choose to live. It didn't have to affect our love as family. He asked if we could agree to disagree, and if we could make more of an effort to stay connected.

I was hardly breathing when he hung up. I sat with the phone in my hand, listening to the dial tone. His wife *knew*? I thought of being fifteen and wanting to kill myself. I'd fallen in love with Zanni in high school while still in a relationship with Javier, and I was so confused, I couldn't take it. I never would have dreamed I could talk to my stepmom about it. If she knew I was gay, did that mean being gay was real and I'm not just messed up? Was it something you can recognize, like being tall? Or athletic? I had so many questions.

My dad said he loved me.

Did that mean God loved me, too?

My dad.

God.

Me.

Suddenly, I began to sob.

* * *

Sometimes I wanted to get as far away as I could. That's when I'd head to Chicago, to see creative friends who were musicians and artists in the city. One friend, Rose, sang at open mic nights and dated interesting people—male, female, different races—all artists. Two albums, Tracy Chapman's "Fast Car" and Tori Amos' "Little Earthquakes" seemed the soundtrack of her world. She was the one who had encouraged me to move away from home and go away to college—to figure out who I was without my family. She'd done it, I could too!

I felt insanely independent when I took the train downtown to visit Rose. We'd stay at her apartment, drink and smoke weed and wander about outside, being young. The city night and its noises enveloped me with hope that there was something, somewhere out there for me.

I had plenty of attractive female friends like Rose who I was not attracted to. I loved them sincerely, but never had romantic feelings for them. There were no complications.

Traveling to what seemed the far away world of the city and hanging with her in the refuge of our friendship was a welcome vacation from my life.

At a party one night, Rose saw me flirting with and following one of her male friends to a couch in the back room. She asked me what I was doing, because I'd already come out to her and there I was playing with this boy—flirting and kissing and leading him on. "What are you doing?!" Rose demanded. I told her I was going to sleep with him, just to make sure I was gay. Truth is, I was desperate for connection and men were easy. I needed to be seen, to be wanted. I had discovered a pattern of events that could distract me when I was hurting. It always started with drinking, followed by 'see me, touch me, hold me, make me real'.

I used to think that being a gay woman meant being incapable of having sex with men. I had been taught many times that being a lesbian meant no men would ever want me, that sex with a man would repulse me and send me lurching in dry heaves. None of those things were ever true for me, and it baffled me. How could I be gay with guys looking at me and checking me out the way they did? I was still in love with my high school girlfriend, didn't want to be gay without her—she had my heart.

Was I to stand around as a single gay girl, turning down perfectly nice boys to boldly defy the world judging me and damning me a queer? Was I to hold court, answering questions that exposed my intimate life? No, thank you. If I couldn't have Zanni, I didn't want the title, the stigma, or any of it. She was the only one I had been willing to take on the world for.

So, I pursued boys, most of the time. Boys would buy me drinks, and alcohol had become my one true and consistent lover. Boys were the easiest bridge to booze, and if I broke up a couple gaining access to his wallet in the course of an evening, I could talk my way out of a fight with her and then sleep with him. Easy peasy. The world wanted to believe that being gay was simple, concise, cut and dry. "It's a choice," people said. Straight or gay, no in between. Gay was a choice made by the lost and perverted. My heart didn't feel perverted, but I did feel lost. I would pray, "What do I need to do? *Show me!*"

With no guidance to go on, I'd decided that if I had a penis as company, I would be in God's better favors. I suppose I preferred the status of heterosexual slut to being a queer. I believed that God and I had a chance at reconciliation with the heterosexual slut selection. I saw heterosexual sluts all the time and figured it was a lifestyle God allowed. I never saw Christians grimacing and holding, "God hates heterosexual sluts!" posters outside nightclubs or marching in parades.

In society's eyes at that time, to be queer was to be fully disenfranchised from God's grace. The way I'd learned it, I was going straight to hell. There were no questions to ask, no conversations to be had, no considerations afforded. Inquiries might have resulted in aggressive silence or violence. If you were in love with someone of the same gender, you were broken, deviant, defiant, to be disposed of. Period.

Naturally, many like me worked to hide being gay by any means necessary. Being gay is about much more than sex and gender. It's about insight, intuition, wisdom and vision. In addition to denying our hearts longing and our authentic lived experience, we also needed to maintain the perpetual masks and emotional crutches that ease the blow of living a lie. I used alcohol. I drank too much and found myself in one-night stands with people I didn't know or care for. That string of brief, impersonal encounters felt dirtier and nastier than any moment I ever spent loving a girl. Loving a woman was the purest, most tender thing I ever experienced.

It was the summer of 1996. After a series of insane relationships, learning that I would need to be in school for two more years to complete my degree, and being the target of hate mail and death threats, I decided to spend the summer far from campus. I stayed at my friend Rory's house. Her family was absolutely calm and normal. I needed some uneventful, drama-free time to wind down.

Rory's mother cooked everything from scratch and her dad belonged to a country club, playing golf with various accounting clients he served in a downtown high rise. Rory had brothers and a home they all grew up in together until they married and moved out. Her parents adored me, and when I said I needed a summer retreat, I was offered the guest room and proceeded to move in for the summer. At twenty-three years old, I welcomed a place that forced me to use my manners and watch my mouth. I would even tiptoe like a naughty teenager when I got in late because I didn't want to wake Rory's parents.

When I came out to Rory, she thought I was kidding. She really thought I was pulling her leg. It was one of the hardest confessions I ever made, because if it freaked her out, I would have died. She made sure I wasn't kidding and then told me she loved me just the same. I was dating Bree, a woman who bartended at Temptations, the lesbian bar I'd staked out years before and more recently made a habit of frequenting. Bree exuded joy and bubbly energy. She was full of life. Her smile hit like the burst of an old cube-flash-camera. She was older and she had a small son. She flirted with me every time I came in. She would smile, bring me a drink, and say something like, "So when are you going to let me take you out and treat you the way you deserve to be treated?"

I agreed to be the designated driver one night, because Bree had some friends in town and didn't want to be responsible. She wanted to have fun! I wanted to go and say happy birthday to Bo before we went out. He was turning eighteen, living by himself in the same trailer park Josh lived in with his wife and sons. We stopped in for a beer and a happy birthday song before going out. I didn't drink much, but I did drink. My tolerance was so high at that time in my life, I figured a couple of drinks didn't matter.

Later, we were facing closing time and I got a hold of some marijuana, which I was happy to smoke as if it were a Marlboro. We said goodbye and exchanged niceties before we headed for the car. I was tired, but I felt fine to drive. We talked the whole way back to Bree's apartment. When we came to an intersection near her place, I paused to let her finish part of a story. When I put my foot on the gas again, all I heard was her gasp in horror. She was staring through me out the driver's side window. I turned to look...

Three days later, when the Demerol wore off, I found myself in a hospital room full of balloons and cards I didn't remember receiving. The TV was on and balloons bounced slightly in the circulating institutional air. My mother was there, happy to see my eyes open. She ran to my bedside and put her hands in front of my face but didn't touch me. She paused them mid-air and said, "Does it hurt?" She had tears in her eyes, and I wanted to grab her hand, but I couldn't move my arm.

"Mom, it's okay. I'm okay." The look on her face told me I was not aware of the condition I was in. Tears were falling and she put her hands on the bars on the side of my bed.

"Where are my brothers?"

"They're here, honey. They've already been in to see you, but it was hard for them to look at you."

"Why?" She twisted her face to keep from crying more, but it didn't work.

"Mom? Why?"

"It's just hard for them to see you like this. But they're here. The doctors said you're very lucky, Jen."

"Mom, I'm thirsty."

"They said they didn't think you were going to make it once they extracted you from the vehicle."

"What do you mean?"

She touched my forehead and moved my hair out of my face. "They said that you surviving is a miracle."

"What happened? Where's Bree?"

"You were in an accident, honey. You got hit by a drunk driver. Bree is alive, but she has a lot of stitches in her face."

"But we were almost to her apartment."

"I know."

It was an eye-opening time, but I still wasn't really paying attention. I learned that the paramedics had pulled me out of the car with the Jaws of Life. The vehicle I was driving was totaled when I was struck in the driver side door by a man driving 60 mph. My body broke as I sat partially where the console had been and partly in the driver's seat, hands still reaching toward the wheel. My midsection was forced to my right around the door that had been bashed in. Bree had hit her face on the dashboard, and because she wore glasses, she had been virtually unrecognizable before they stitched her up. She had taken some insane amount of stitches to her face muscles and skin.

The man who hit us was in his 60s. He was the breadwinner for a family of two or three generations that he supported. He had lost his job that afternoon and then sat drinking in the parking lot all night. At four o'clock the next morning he was sufficiently intoxicated to have the nerve to head home and face his family. He flew out of the parking lot without headlights, thinking the industrial park area would be empty at that time of morning. He blew through the intersection, and I stopped him.

My girlfriend sued and made out quite well, but I decided not to sue. Call me an idiot, but I didn't feel right about the idea. I could not ignore the fact that this man hit two women in a car, and we were mangled at the intersection while he was drunk out of his mind. There was no one around and not only would he have gotten away, but there would have been no witnesses. He did the right thing anyway. He called 911 and stayed until they arrived. And I got to live.

I thank God my dad had insurance that paid for the hospital, the ambulance, and the machines I was connected to. I fractured three ribs and punctured a lung that was operating at only twenty percent capacity. There was an inch-long slit in my right side where a tube was inserted between two ribs to drain my lung of internal bleeding. My entire torso was so bruised that I had to grab pens and crawl my fingers around to scratch itches. All of the muscles above my knees were on fire with pain any time I moved.

My father and I had the first open conversation about alcohol when I recovered from that accident. He shared his belief that alcohol is the Devil. We spoke about alcoholism and how powerful it is—ending relationships, families, and lives. I was lucky to walk away from the wreck. I tried to bond with my dad over church, writing and college—our greatest bond to this day is one that I'd have never wanted to forge. My dad and I both cannot drink alcohol.

I was beginning to recognize how precious life is and how quickly it can be taken away. I thought of the most important people in my life and their impact on my world. One person in particular came to mind. I had run into my fifth-grade teacher multiple times through the years. After being in her class I stood up in her wedding, and we'd bump into each other at the mall sometimes, or, after her divorce she would invite me over to the house to visit so she could check on me. She always knew that the world I lived in conflicted with the world that lived in me.

I knew that she lived across the street from where I had lived when I was in her class years before. It was nearing the December holidays, so I wrote a heartfelt Christmas card detailing many moments that her caring and kindness had held me together. I told her how her presence had truly altered the school life experience of an otherwise very confused little girl. I decided to hand deliver the note, hoping to catch her at home and visit.

When nobody answered after multiple doorbell rings, I put the card in her mailbox. Her neighbor opened the door and asked if she could help, and I told her I was looking for Carla, that I was a former student. The neighbor smiled. "Her students love her, don't they?! Sweetheart, Ms. Belser's been sick; I think she's at the doctor today. Can I tell her you came by?" I wanted to see her so badly that I thought I'd like to wait, but then her neighbor would just watch me standing there, so I told her my name and pointed out that I was leaving a card. I made sure to mention that my phone number was inside, and I'd love for Carla to call.

A few weeks later she did call, and it was the first time I'd heard her voice in years. She called me by my last name and that tickled me to death. "I got your card; I'm sorry I missed you."

"I'm glad you got it."

I always got self-conscious when I spoke with her, her approval meant the world to me. I noticed that this time felt a little different—I was an adult. I began to appreciate that this was an opportunity to be friends with her as a grown woman and wondered what that would look like. I was scared of her knowing that I smoked cigarettes, or that I drank like I did. I was scared of her knowing I was gay. And yet I wanted her to know all of it. With her approval, I could finally determine whether I was worthy of love or not. I decided to light a cigarette, and she heard the click of the lighter through the phone.

"Jennifer, are you smoking?!"

"Yeah, I picked up the habit years ago." Part of me remembered her smoking and felt the beginnings of an adult kinship with her over the destructive habit.

"Oh, Jennifer. I hoped that you were smarter than that. I wish I never smoked."

"I won't smoke forever. It's just where I'm at right now." I went on to tell her about the car accident, and how just as all the court stuff ended for that, my favorite aunt was hit by a truck and placed in an induced coma, having suffered substantial brain damage and internal bleeding. Carla asked me about school, and I asked how she and her son, Ryan, were doing.

"You know, Ryan and I are moving this month. I want to have you over when we settle in, so you can see how big my baby boy is, and I can see you with my own two eyes."

I was thrilled. We spoke for a while longer and she gave me a phone number where I could reach her in two months, and we'd set up a dinner date from there. I couldn't wait. I was both relieved and terrified that I was going to finally have the opportunity to come out to my most trusted adult. I wanted so badly for her to accept me, but even if she didn't, I just needed to know. I placed her number in my jewelry box for safe keeping. I hoped and prayed that the visit would go well.

* * *

In the back of my mind I always hoped that my high school girlfriend would come around. I pined for Zanni well into my twenties, always expecting that when she got worn down by bad relationships, she would concede what a good match we were and come back to me.

On one level, everything I was doing was to make her proud of me. If I were honest, I was just biding my time until she returned. I was living my plan B. Sometimes throughout college she would call, and I imagined she would finally admit that I had been right all along.

Toward the end of my six years in school she agreed to visit. I just knew it was time. Life had finally worn her down. She was willing to confess that I was right; I was her one and only true love.

She arrived and at twenty-four years old, I felt fifteen again. All of the mistakes I'd made were going to be wiped from existence. Our story was about to pick up where it had left off. We would make love, the stars would align again, she'd be there for my graduation, and we'd grow old together...

Shortly after Zanni arrived, we found ourselves fumbling around in the bedroom. Awkward. When we finished, she had to go. The woman who left me that day looked familiar but was a complete stranger. There was no connection, no resurrection of hope. There would be no cleaning of the slate or growing old together. I had to face myself.

I lay naked in a bed that held no answers. I stared at the ceiling, numb. If the dream of her and I didn't exist, then who was I?

Zanni never came back to me, and today I thank her. I believe she came to see me at college that day entirely for herself—that she found herself lost, and the mess we had been was the last positive vestige of her identity that she was willing to claim. Moments of looking into each other's eyes in our youth, we had both been hopeful that we could save each other from all we'd been through. I believe she came that last time because like me, she needed to see if we were true. If she could find herself worthy of fighting for.

The last place Zanni had seen herself and trusted it, had been in my eyes. She knew that I had loved her and believed in her. There was a time when I truly thought I would die if she didn't stay.

Today, I choose to believe that she did love me—as best she could. The ardent hope I carried for so long scared her; she'd already been burdened with more shame than she could breathe through, and our love was a vulnerable place she could not survive within. She had to shut down to find her way out. She saw my tattered wings, recognized them. I trust that I was right about her, and she could see me through the scars. She knew we could have been together and nursed our pain, or that she could push me out of the nest. Maybe I give her too much credit, but it's how I need to tell my story to keep the memory of young love gentle. Whatever the case, I trust that she knew I was strong enough to repair myself one day. And then I would fly. For both of us.

CHAPTER NINE

When I was growing up, kids used to call people alcoholic like they called people crazy or gay. There was no awareness that these conditions existed as complicated matters; only that they were great put-downs. I thought drinking was normal and drinking too much was funny. Drinking too much was forgivable. Drinking and behaving badly was also forgivable, but none of those things should be spoken about outside the home. I learned that incidents and embarrassing moments can happen when drunk, and drinking makes telling lies okay.

Making promises and not keeping them was another behavior that frequently aligned itself with my drinking, but the rule of thumb was that life worked better when it never got discussed. "Incidents" didn't happen all the time, and there were a lot of happy moments in between. The rule was clear—focus on good things when speaking outside the home and keep the bad things inside. That is where I struggled. The bad things always stayed inside me and haunted me. Those emotions lingered and the only way I could be free was to drink. It was a never-ending cycle of denial and self-medication to cope with what we couldn't bring to light. Alcoholism makes families sick.

As my addiction to alcohol progressed, I habitually didn't stop drinking until I'd chalked up more irresponsible behavior that only drinking would numb. I was in a repeat phase long before I recognized the pattern. I was drinking to escape the sense of powerlessness I'd learned through being sexualized early, compounded by witnessing traumatic fights as a little girl, and having my family split down the middle. Everyone in the family adopted roles and communication styles that shielded them while perpetuating confusion and dysfunction. We were all missing each other in an effort to avoid pushing buttons.

Nobody wanted to rock the boat, but everyone was uncomfortable. No one learns autonomy without having an impact on others.

A person can't live from their own moral compass when there is only one compass for the family and its magnet is broken.

I had no one around to turn to in my confusion, and my young adulthood suffered from symptoms caused by a childhood of hiding the truth, silence, and loneliness. It took tremendous work to let go of feeling stupid, clumsy, and incompetent with all of the rules I had to discern for myself.

When I was graduating college in 1998 from the school my father went to—the reason I went, the graduation he failed to attend—my older brother was going through a divorce. Josh rarely reached out to me, but he had been calling me for about a week and a half, crying on the phone. He'd wanted to break the pattern of divorce. Of drinking. He wanted to be a father to his boys, buy a plot of land and build a house with them so they'd have their own mud to squish their toes in. He felt he'd failed. For whatever reason, their relationship was ending, and he needed to find a place to live—he was going to leave the boys in their home, thinking that was best for them.

I'd never been the one Josh leaned on, but I wanted to help. Though I'd wanted nothing more for the last ten years than to live in the city among gay people and become a performer, I suggested that Josh and I get a place together temporarily. We could help each other out financially until we both got on our feet. He agreed.

We knew a guy who would sell us a house in Aurora. Josh wanted a place his two sons could call home. He didn't want an apartment. I said I would sign the mortgage, but only stay for two years. He said okay. We moved. It was a beautiful ranch home in a ritzy cul-de-sac in the suburbs. I got the master bedroom with my own bathroom. We had a backyard, a beautiful deck the full length of the house, trellis sides. A shed, garage, basketball hoop, laundry in the house, front lawn to mow. At first, I really liked it. I liked that Josh and I were getting close. He began to experience first-hand some of the painful realities I dealt with being a lesbian. We actually talked about it. He encouraged me to come out at my first job in Lombard, because there was a lot of homophobic shit going on at work and I was really uncomfortable.

Josh got a girlfriend and started spending a lot of time with her. I got depressed because I was alone in suburbia and knew no one. Josh noticed my depression one of the few times I saw him that month, and he offered to pay for my first class at Second City because he knew that was what I wanted to be doing. I made the commute to Chicago every Saturday for class.

I met Conner and Doug, and many others. Conner was a minister's kid too. We clicked right away. Doug drank as much as we did. It became routine that everyone would meet after class at The Last Act, across the street from Second City. Most of the class would file out within a couple hours, and the three of us would inevitably close the bar. Then we would go back to Conner's apartment and drink until we all passed out. It would usually take until five or six in the morning, after a case of post-bar drinking.

I eventually came out of the closet to everyone and that made me feel sometimes better and sometimes too vulnerable. I was nervous with every scene I participated in that maybe people would think something weird if I did this or that, and they would think it was because I was gay. I left classes so anxious that I would drink like a madwoman to mute it all.

Eventually, Conner and I became sexual. We had talked about it, and neither of us was interested in the other, not sexually anyway. But we loved each other (or the companionship of a fellow drinker) as friends, so it worked out well. There were never any strings attached. Never anything to answer to in the morning. That went on for about a year. Every now and then, he'd call. "Whatcha doin? Wanna watch a football game and get some beers, and maybe have sex later?"

"Okay."

And that's what we did. I didn't care. I didn't want it to matter. I just wanted to drink alcohol and have sex.

While I didn't ever have to answer to Conner, I always obsessed over what the hell it meant. Was I really gay? Should I date men? Was I just sick of all the heartache with women? Had I really felt love for any of the women I'd been with since Zanni?

In hindsight, I believe I was madly in love with every single one of them, for a spell. But if I wasn't able to define myself in a healthy way that felt correct, how could I ever begin to make a life for myself or a life to share? I drove myself mad. The pressure I felt eventually affected Conner and he could not get it up even for meaningless sex. He confessed that knowing I was not attracted to his body made his body unresponsive. Both he and that arrangement eventually proved futile.

I created distractions—chaos that was enough to stay lost in for a brief time, until it wasn't. Then I'd do it again. I was always kicking up dirt to camouflage what I didn't know how to process. I would do anything to avoid sitting still with myself. Mostly I'd just listen to music, write, and use extensive amounts of weed and alcohol.

When I returned home from the city, Josh hadn't been home all weekend. I was living alone in a house we had gotten together, mostly for him. We hadn't signed the mortgage yet; the guy had given us three months to come up with the money. At the end of three months, I told Josh I couldn't do it. I would end up resenting him and I didn't want that. I wasn't happy—I had to move to the City sooner than waiting two years. (After all, that's where my drinking buddies were). Otherwise I would smoke weed and drink all night in that house by myself.

I'd begun a sexual relationship with a married woman at work. She was fucking crazy in lust with me. We would go to her house on our lunch break for a quickie and sometimes we had sex at work. I was insane.

The women I'd become involved with often expressed being in awe of me. Their adoration was a magical replacement for self-esteem. I seemed to awaken something in them. They would tell me, "Jen, there's just something about you," or "You exude this sexual energy." They'd confess that they'd never felt this way before. I believed them because I remembered that feeling. Seeing the discovery in their eyes kept me alive. I'd play the role of confidence to keep them near, but mostly, I felt like nobody wanted the real me, and I knew their interest would only quell the ache for a short time.

I was nothing they'd ever known to be true about lesbians. I had long hair, wore make-up, spoke of loving God, and I had even been with men. I represented a whole new world to them, a world in which women could be more than a wife or a mother or arm candy. Women could buck the system and be beautiful, strong, in charge, and courageous—to them I was.

For a long time, I was a needy child, seeking connection anywhere I could find some kind attention. I pity the girl I was during that time. She was lost. She wanted to belong to someone and feel the safety she had felt when she and God used to hang out.

Josh was disappointed that we wouldn't keep the house, but he said it was fine. We agreed to get an apartment and I help pay for a few months, so I went apartment searching.

It wasn't long until a friend of a friend recommended a nice two-bedroom apartment that was available. Josh and I both signed the lease, although he lived primarily with his girlfriend. He had to work a lot of hours on his job. When he got visitation of his boys on Sundays, I was happy to step in and watch them until he got off work. Those two boys and their curious, creative energy were the bright spot in my life. I always looked forward to being with them.

I continued taking classes downtown and drinking like mad. I was past the point of drinking for the taste. After work you'd find me smoking on a balcony that overlooked rolling green hills of suburban apartment living. We were just above a crystal-blue kidney shaped pool that sparkled refreshingly in the moon and parking lot lights. I wondered if I stood on my porch railing and dove toward the pool if I'd hit water or ground. I thought of my nephews.

Sitting in our apt with the lights off, I'd stare through the TV set, drowning my depression with warm gin from the bottle. I prayed to pass out before I could effectively attempt suicide. While everything was feeling hopeless, I still wanted to live.

Sometimes I got together with an old, married boyfriend. We would go out drinking and end up talking about if things had been different. We would go back to my apartment and have sex that I didn't remember having afterward. Sometimes I knew the person I brought home, other times I didn't.

I met my neighbors downstairs, and they liked to party. The music suggested that they partied often, so I started going downstairs to bum a cigarette, intending to use their stash. We would smoke blunts and drink and listen to crazy music. I had sex with one of them in a locked room while his girlfriend was banging on the door, threatening to kill me. When we finished, he jumped up to go and console her. He left me in the room and wished me luck in my escape because she knew where I lived.

I ran home and locked the door, then passed out on the kitchen floor with my back against the door. When I awoke the next day, my head was killing me. I had a moment of clarity. I could see myself and I hated who I'd become. What a mess.

* * *

When I was in college, I met a most intriguing gay couple, Poe and Jerry. They were intellectuals, writers, and practicing Christians. They were out of the closet at work, on the college campus, and they still called themselves Christians. I was riveted.

There were times in the midst of my madness during those years when I was ashamed or frightened or lonely, that I would call one of them up as a surrogate to God. Poe and Jerry adored me; they saw the pressure I was under on and off campus in the local community as The Lesbian Advocate. They knew I was young and newly outed through my comic strip, so they trusted I had too much to carry. They always invited me over to talk. They made dinner for me and a date once, and I had the opportunity to ask questions about becoming a writer, a professor, and also a Christian. I was interested in all of those things.

That evening at their apartment, talking about Christianity with two men who loved each other and loved Jesus planted a seed in me. The aroma of dinner cooking, warm-colored décor, a worn Bible on the coffee table and lit candles created a cozy atmosphere that attached to the idea of God and Gay co-existing. Their conviction was so clear—in both their identity as gay men and their identity in

Christ—that I left with even more information to wade through. The most important part is that Poe told me while he hugged me goodbye that God loved me and had a plan for my life, and that I was good. I kept their phone number after I graduated college and carried it with me for years as a grain of hope. A lifeline.

I was wasted the evening I dialed that long-distance number. I slurred through my receiver that I didn't want to live anymore; I couldn't stand myself. I told Poe I couldn't hold onto a relationship to save my life, that I couldn't hold a job. I had nothing left but alcohol and it was going to kill me. I told him that God was so disappointed in me that I needed him to do me a huge favor. I asked him if he would pray and put in a good word for me, to please tell God I was trying, and I didn't know what else to do. I told him I called because he was a gay Christian, and I hoped he could tell me why I felt so insane and hopeless.

His response has never left me.

Calmly and warmly, he asked me to sit down and listen. I sat down and held the receiver with two hands for dear life. He told me that God had given me so many gifts, and I was hurting and miserable because I had been acting ungrateful. God wanted me to use the gifts he gave me, and I wouldn't find peace until I did.

That night I didn't want to be alone, so I went over to a friend's house to watch a movie with her family. I drank a twelve-pack before going. I sat on the floor between their 'his and hers' chairs while she folded laundry. His socks. This pile. Her panties. That pile. Her son's jeans. Over there.

The tricky thing about shame is that everything and nothing at all can ignite it. Instead of enjoying a movie and relaxing, I wanted a drink. Her life was so normal; by contrast I felt like a pathetic freak. I didn't have his and hers chairs and never will. I don't have kids' stuff and never will. I'm just a lonely gay woman with no real prospect for future partnership. Shame loves the unspoken triggers because they are everywhere, and they bind perfectly with self-centered pity. Shame wins.

I was squirming with discomfort, and finally got up to go. I ran out of the house and into the driveway to leave. I needed to get as far away from there as I could. I went home and called my college friend Henry who lived in Minneapolis, a man well learned in my drinking. I told Henry I was coming out. It was 1:30 a.m. He asked if I'd been drinking. I said no.

My brother gave me a map, cell phone, and a nervous glance, knowing that once I had set my mind to something...I jumped in my car and on that trip, I drove off the rode twice falling asleep at the wheel. I had two cups of coffee and about five caffeine pills, but I hadn't slept all night, and I was fighting that sleepy haze that comes when drinks are wearing off.

I drove through the night and into the morning, my mind obsessing the whole way. As I approached the St. Paul skyline, I called Henry to say I was almost there. At that moment my heart began to race, I felt clammy. I dropped the phone. I had smoked about two packs of cigarettes on the drive, not to mention before I'd left. I pulled my car to the shoulder and stood watching the skyline, certain it was the last thing I'd ever see. I was convinced I was having a heart attack. My face, chest, fingers, belly, and arms were numb. I was banging on my chest, trying to make something work.

Henry calmly talked me down from panic over the phone. When I got to his house, I called into work for three days, claiming a friend of mine from high school had pulled a spontaneous marriage in Minneapolis and I wasn't going to miss it for the world. Ridiculous yet plausible stories fell from my lips all the time to justify my erratic behavior. I left that message on my boss's machine and went to sleep for the next nine hours.

When I woke up, I didn't know where I was. After a few minutes, the horror of the night before began to play across my mind. Watching the movie of my life without alcohol in me was torture. I didn't know how much longer I could stand to take responsibility for the things my shadow side did while drinking. I was too ashamed to claim my life.

I proceeded for three days to divorce myself from reality and my responsibilities. I read a book called *Mere Christianity*. Henry had found God. He and I had always philosophized about it in college, but he'd really found God again, and I could see he was at tremendous peace. He suggested the book and I read it. We talked. I walked. I drank and obsessed. I drove home.

I returned to work and because they adored me, my greatest punishment was suffering ridicule for not taking pictures of my best friend's wedding. At home, I flipped dumbly through a Bible and read another recommended book, *Your God is Too Small.* I watched Oprah incessantly, twice each day. I pulled out a blue book I had gotten from an AA meeting once. I read feverishly, drink in hand, searching for the key to get out of my mess. I was losing my mind.

When the apartment lease was ending, I quickly found a new place on the North Side of Chicago. I was sure things would get better once I was out of a holding pattern and actually pursuing my dream. I worked my job for another month until the commute kicked my ass, and then told them I was going to work for Second City. (Liar. I had a graphic design project for the Chicago Improv Festival, but that was a small contract.) They said they were sorry to see me go.

I moved into a gorgeous three-story brick apartment building on Argyle Street with a forty-one-year-old Japanese gay man. Within hours of moving in I knew that he was on antidepressants, he was a practicing Buddhist, he was single but dating, a published author, and a non-smoker.

The woodwork in the apartment was beautiful and he had the space decorated simply; it invited my personal growth. There were plants, and it was organized and clean. I was able to have my own room and set up my computer in the dining room. We had a back porch, and he intently conveyed our mutual responsibility for keeping the space clean. I knew I could do well there, although his calm demeanor was a sharp contrast for the raw alcoholic girl, I hid from him in our interview.

My new housemate was playful as a six-year-old, and he would spend his time off surfing the web for a husband. We got along well enough, once I learned how to live around him. I began writing, which consisted of sitting at my computer, starting it up, typing a few words, and then taking a break on the back porch. The break would last for hours—

drinking whiskey, smoking cigarettes, and talking on the phone. I had broken ties with the married woman and was going to start over.

Josh went to his high school reunion and told me a girl I knew in high school had asked about me and seemed interested in getting in touch. I got her address and wrote to her. She was cute. Maybe it was fate. She responded. She came out to visit, and asked me since Suzanne was officially out of the picture, would I be her girlfriend? Genuinely tickled, I said yes.

We dated for about a month and a half. She lived in the suburbs and I drove out to see her as often as possible. She worked in a hospital. She knew a woman who was having a year-long sexual liaison with a hot little twenty-five-year-old. She had had many discussions with this woman as to whether the affair meant she was gay.

The hot little twenty-five -year-old was me. The friend was the married woman I had finally ended it with. It wasn't the most comfortable discovery as I was lying naked in the arms of a new relationship. I felt like a whore. She said don't worry about it.

When we went out, we drank. She didn't want to have sex with me. That frustrated me. I was a mess and trying to make sense of who I was. I projected my insecurities a lot and did it with her. To me, anyone I was friendly with could become a sexual partner. Sadly, that had been my experience. Since her best friend was a guy, I accused her of infidelity. She drank more. We fought. We drank. We fought.

I called her one day at work. I didn't say anything but hello, we need to talk. She said she knew we weren't working, and good luck. That was it.

* * *

I lived in Chicago for five years before moving to Los Angeles. I found my share of tumult; the source varied—relationships, pursuit of fame and fortune, employment, and where I chose to live. Oh yeah, and the 9/11 attacks on New York.

I was involved with three beautiful women in Chicago: Elsa, Yuji, and Daya. They were all creatives—a writer, a musician, and an actress, respectively. I was drawn to the brokenness of Elsa, the writer, and her capacity to portray to the world something larger than her pain. I admired how anger and escape drove her to produce new material. She was also an editor, and impossible to reach emotionally. We were okay only when she chose to approach. She would move in and adore me, ravish me, then return to business as usual. I think she intrigued me because she had the audacity to identify as a bisexual woman. She'd recently ended a long-term relationship with a man, and his picture remained on the refrigerator and book shelves while we explored each other.

The apartment in Chicago felt like a museum, longing for a day that was dead and gone. Old lace dresses and dry flowers adorned the walls. *This American Life* on NPR fought static through an old radio with two face knobs. Elsa fried chicken in a skillet. She asked too many questions. Her interest in my most private thoughts both attracted and offended me. She would carry my feelings and circumstances like props into her writing and graft them to another character's story. She wanted to move to New York, and I grew excited, because it sounded magical to leave and start over again. She wanted to go without me.

Elsa initiated our relationship, then boldly insisted that she could never fully commit to me. What I heard was, 'I'm afraid to be gay.' That is not what she said, but it was all I was able to hear. It fell into my self-destructive comfort zone, because what I wanted was once again out of reach. I begged her to say I was enough for her. I knew I could compete with another woman, but not with a man. We have different things to offer, plain and simple.

Bisexual? I couldn't make sense of it! I'd convinced myself that bisexuals were not real. I decided it was a transitional phase between living straight and being honest about being gay. It signified a need to make a decision, to get off the fence. I was perplexed by the unorthodox resolution she carried regarding her sexual orientation. I felt it my duty to protect gay women everywhere by drop-kicking her straddled confidence and rightfully landing her into one of the two boxes I believed in. Straight or gay.

I wanted to find a woman who was a clear-cut lesbian. No more bisexuality or confused women for me. I'd had enough of that; I was drawing the line. I'd spent years in college defending my right to love women and felt it necessary to stand behind it. Many women I crossed paths with had recently been in relationships with men or were still in complicated situations with men. I told myself that I had come out of the closet very young, and it was understandable that some women in their early 30s were just coming out.

The second relationship in Chicago was the musician, Yuji. We met online and the first date went poorly, because she spoke of her ex the whole time. On the second date, I went to a bar to see her sing with her band, and it was obsession at first sight. I was not only moved by her music; I completely fell for the idea of her. She and I quickly became enmeshed. I often felt afraid because she wanted very much to be with me and only me. This was new territory, marking the beginning of my post-college journey, and a lesson that lesbian relationships could actually be monogamous and publicly acknowledged without the imminent threat of bodily harm.

Yuji and I loved as big as we fought. We cycled through seasons of peace and mutual support that would eventually crash into volatile and emotionally abusive storms. We could be calm and tender, or angry and cruel. Inside, we both walked the wire precariously above our soul sickness and behaved with kindness in spite of it; but when we lacked the stamina to suppress our pain and behave well, the rage flew out of us and at each other. We were doing the best we knew how to do. She made beautiful music to remain sane, and I was finding my way in comedy theater. Eventually I stopped hiding and apologizing for drinking too much. She would at times disappear from behind her eyes—go far inside herself for refuge. One day we got in a fight so intense that she fled town and didn't contact me for weeks. Ultimately, I decided it qualified as a break up. I was so exhausted, and I'd left several messages. What else could I do?

I was far too insecure and attractive to stay single for long. Friends had been wanting to set me up with a local actress, Daya, and they introduced us the first chance they got. I first saw her on stage rehearsing and although she wasn't the lead, her character stole my attention.

Daya was refreshingly calm and measured. She was easy to engage with; flirting with her was simple. She too held great sadness but was far more guarded. It didn't spill from her. She used it to strengthen her posture. She exuded a confidence that I was not familiar with but wanted to emulate. By day, Daya was a modern professional woman and by night a thespian revealing yoga sculpted limbs in bed. The sex was sensational, and I grew to admire her for many reasons.

When I learned that she took antidepressants it blew the top off all assumptions I'd made about people who needed medication. She recognized the way I ruminated in my mind, how I was a victim of my own mental warfare. She understood the way my thoughts assaulted and exhausted me. I couldn't stop thinking. She said I should see her doctor.

I drank alcohol and smoked weed to mute the inner chaos and find some peace. By the time I was with Daya, I was nearing the end of my mental rope. Drinking wasn't consistently effective anymore. I never knew which drunk I'd become that night or whether I'd remember anything I did. I might be fun, funny, quiet, sad, angry, or an asshole. I always did things I later regretted, and I couldn't control it. Once, alcohol had been my solution to feeling uncomfortable in my skin. Now it controlled me. I couldn't be sure if alcohol was driving me crazy or keeping me from it. It didn't matter anymore how I had gotten here. The house was on fire and I needed to leave.

I made small efforts to save my life, which I kept to myself. One example was entering a women's bookstore on the North Side of Chicago and asking for any books they had about alcoholism. I had used the term for years to describe myself so that I could avoid appearing ignorant to folks about the amount I could drink in an evening. I used the term to justify the way I drank, to own it, and sadly it had become a badge of honor. But at this point the honor had worn off. I was out of my mind and hoped to God there was an explanation somewhere in that bookstore.

The woman who worked there searched both computer and shelves before claiming to have found only one book that spoke about alcoholism. She said it was a memoir/self-help book. *Drinking: A Love Story* by Caroline Knapp. I bought it and read it in one sitting, then read it a second time. I was both horrified and relieved at how much I related to her story. I felt a little less alone yet kept the revelation to myself. I knew I needed to change how I was living, but there had to be some way that I could manage my drinking better. I couldn't imagine stopping. Never again?

Daya had a doctor who helped her. I noted that she still smoked weed. Maybe I wouldn't need to quit drinking entirely. Maybe medication could help me to drink more sensibly. I quickly abandoned my moral stand against drug companies and became open to the idea.

Daya took antidepressants. She was beautiful and successful, sexy and smart. She was funny and tender, she laughed and cried. Maybe I could be like that. She gave me her doc's number and I decided to call.

CHAPTER TEN

The city was still abnormally tense with threats of post 9-11 anthrax in the mail. Many stories circulated, like the one that there were biochemical agents aboard the planes when they hit the towers in New York, and killer chemicals would find their way across the globe through the air. On some level I think everyone was waiting to start gasping and frothing at the mouth because of some biochemical agents we heard about on the nightly news. I worked downtown at the Sun-Times building when the planes hit. When I arrived at work, we all gathered around one woman's small black and white TV, trying to make sense of what was happening.

There had grown an eeriness I'd never experienced in my beloved city. Parades of people marching silently along sidewalks with cell phones to their ears and their eyes fixed on the sky. Bank lines stretched around the corner and occasionally in an otherwise noisy city, you might hear a sneeze or cough above an ambulance in the distance.

As a cigarette smoker, I'd take breaks and ride down the elevator to talk with police officers or security guards who had been assigned to our building. I spoke with one who confessed that they weren't supposed to speak to us. I asked him why so many extra officers had suddenly appeared. Why were they there? He said plainly, "I don't know. To provide the illusion of security?" I asked him what he was trained to do if a plane were to hit or some aftershock from the attacks in New York were to suddenly present in Chicago. He looked me in the eyes and said, "Very little."

"So, what would you do?" I asked.

"Just like you, I'd run for my life."

The jig was up. I had already suspected that the city had done just that, provided the illusion of security to anxious citizens. I also knew that one man couldn't stop a plane from crashing, bombs dropping, anthrax, or paratroopers. I knew he alone couldn't ward off a truck bomber if they chose to drive into the building. In light of obvious logic, his honesty was appreciated.

I remember the thought crossing my mind: The world is insane, and I can't afford to be in a blackout. Still, I drank heartily. The paranoia and fear consuming a post 9-11 America was added fuel and justification for my drinking.

I sat on the couch, waiting for it to sink in. The doctor sat across from me, asking if I had any questions or concerns. I was waiting for it to become real. I studied his face closely, wondering if I could trust him. Daya did.

Clinically depressed, he'd said. I sat erect in the words, certain I'd be hauled off to an institution, tranquilized and propped up in front of a locked window near an easel. Wearing only a paper robe and slippers, I'd be reduced to finger painting in a roomful of others who'd once had great potential but failed to pull their lives together. I almost welcomed it.

"Jennifer, do you have any questions for me?" He seemed kind and smart. He didn't creep me out. I felt like I could trust him. Still, I was nervous. "Okay, then. I have a few for you."

First, he asked me again about my drinking. I lied and said I drank from time to time. Gratefully, I sensed he knew better. He told me that I may be an alcoholic and to be sure, I needed to stop drinking. He wanted to be able to see if the drinking was causing or medicating the depression, and he couldn't determine that if I continued to drink.

Stop drinking? I thought.

"Do you think you could stop drinking for a while, Jennifer?"

My mind drifted back to a time with Yuji, when I had been forced to stop for a while. It was the night before I moved in with her, and I showed my true colors and became excessively drunk. She asked me to return her keys to the apartment. She said she thought I had a problem and she didn't want to have that problem move into her small space. While I could appreciate that, I was stuck. I had already given my landlord notice; all of my apartment was packed up and three quarters of it had already been moved to her place. The next day, she asked that I come over to discuss it. She told me that I couldn't move in unless I promised not to drink. Startled, I told her I wasn't sure that I could make good on that promise.

Two facts remained; Yuji was not negotiating, and my things were mostly moved in already. I had nowhere else to go, so I conceded. Proud of myself, I awaited her satisfied response. Instead, she looked at me skeptically and said, "I need it in writing."

At first, I thought she was kidding, and I laughed, but I was the only one laughing. She told me she was dead earnest, that I was ugly when I was that drunk and she didn't want that woman to move in. I felt both manipulated and hopeful. Maybe I needed someone like her to keep me in line. Maybe that was what I needed to stay motivated and in control.

I wrote a letter to her, a promise to stay free from alcohol as long as I was in that apartment and in a relationship with her. I meant it.

For six months I didn't touch a drop. I chain-smoked cigarettes until she came down on me for smoking. I'd come home from work and she'd move in close to my face, sniff a few times, and say in disgust, "You smoked today." I felt dirty and ashamed, but I couldn't stop. I received no validation for not drinking. I thought about drinking all the time, but the prospect of being kicked out of the apartment kept me dry.

She wasn't impressed. She just expected me to keep my word.

Perhaps Yuji dreamt that one by one, she would emancipate me from my vices. There may have been a part of her that wanted to see what the mangled doll looked like when she was all cleaned up. Such potential.

To be fair, I think we both harbored some desire to save the other from herself. Her scrutiny left me feeling like a rat in a cage, but I had nowhere to go. I was quietly going mad inside—wildly chasing my tail. Yuji seemed at peace with her band and music, and I felt like I was being sucked back into a loud, dark nothingness. I was suffocating.

I wanted to escape the apartment but was afraid to say I needed space. She might think I'd drink. Eventually, the day came when I couldn't behave any more. I finally got the nerve to do what I felt like doing. Yuji and I were on Clark Street. She was screaming at me about something insensitive I'd done, but I couldn't hear her. Not drinking had drained me of all resources. I'd run into dreadful debt and I was turned inside out. When you drank the way I did for so many years and then just stop, something happens. Images, feelings, truths begin to surface that had been buried deep, for everyone's sake. Things that only whiskey knew how to pin. For months I'd been breaking up fights inside my own head without a liquid referee, and I was numb from exhaustion.

Catatonic silence was my last line of defense against being discovered for the real me—the shame and anger I never dealt with that had penetrated me to the cellular level. I drove on auto pilot that day, Yuji's mouth moving athletically, and her face twisted from abandonment. I felt nothing. Oh, to feel again.

I stopped at a red light, looked at her robotically, then opened the car door and stepped out onto the street. I walked around the open door and up the street. One block, two blocks, three blocks toward the mirage of blinking liquor store lights. If only I could make it...to...that...store... I felt I was slithering along the asphalt, a wounded soldier's crawl desperately dragging his body to refuge—into the liquor store. I ordered a bottle of Jack Daniels, the only one who understood me. I put more money than the bottle cost on the counter and without hesitation began to open it as I exited the store.

In broad Chicago daylight I followed the same course back to my vehicle, cars honking as I poured glorious whiskey down my throat, extinguishing fires and fears. Tears came to my eyes. I gasped and air entered my lungs. I could feel *me* again! Another long draw and like oil on a rusted hinge, I felt smooth again. Color washed over the world, birds returned to the sky, and I could see my car, with a door open, sitting at a stop light and Yuji was looking at me through the windshield. I could see her from a block away, and I chuckled. Was she really still sitting there with the car running? With my door open? I drew again on the bottle. Who cared about Yuji? I could finally exhale. I had what I needed.

Only a crazy woman would get back in that car. Only a crazy woman would walk down a busy street in broad daylight, drinking whiskey from the bottle without enough shame to use a paper bag. I was she. She was me. The crazy lady.

The doctor repeated himself, "You need to stop drinking, Jennifer. Do you think you can do that? I'd like to try you on some medication for your depression, but you need to stop drinking for it to work."

"I'll try."

"You can go to Alcoholics Anonymous if you find that you can't do it by yourself. Have you heard of them? Alcoholics Anonymous?"

I remembered seeing my dad's book on my grandmother's bookshelf in her condo after she died. We'd all been invited to go through her condo and take things that were special to us, to remember her by. I grabbed a green stovetop pan that she used to make tomato soup for grilled cheese sandwiches. I also grabbed a book called Living Sober that my dad had gotten when he chose to stop drinking in the eighties.

I had to stop drinking...Could I? He did. The doc gave me some medication, talked with me about how to take it, and said we'd talk again soon.

* * *

A friend asked me to host a Halloween auction fundraiser at a lesbian bar. She had a higher-paying gig that she was offered and wanted to take. I said sure. I knew I could drink for free at those things and was flattered that she thought of me to cover it. In our small world of lesbian performers, I respected her. The night was fun over all, albeit awkward a time or two when Yuji showed up and my new girl, Daya, was in the room. I just drank more and told more jokes from the stage.

At the end of the night, with no large misgivings, I talked Daya and some friends into hitting one more gay bar uptown that I knew was still open. It was a school night, but I was unemployed. They agreed, and we arrived just before last call.

I ran to the bar and ordered several pitchers for the four of us who had made the trek. The last thing I remember that night before a blackout stole me was the golden liquid glistening, lights from the dance floor behind it, as I playfully raised the pitcher higher and lower to pour. The beautiful, golden, seemingly harmless liquid sparkling in the lights of a club. And...SCENE!

I woke up in my girlfriend's bed on the North Side of Chicago. She was gone to work. It was 1:00 p.m. when I heard the phone ring and answered it. My hangover always made the world sound miles away, even if it was right there, coming through the receiver. I learned a few things from that call. One, that I had forgotten and therefore missed a job interview that morning. Two, that I was supposed to meet Daya for lunch after the interview, to tell her how it went and return her keys; and three, that she was disappointed, but not angry. She never got angry at me, but she told me later that day that she didn't like when I drank as much as I did the night before. She said that I could get mean. When I said I didn't remember anything, it didn't soothe much. I was ashamed. Again.

I'd been having experiences for years that confirmed her observations. I couldn't control my drinking. I would always have to drink more than people saw me drinking. I'd have an extra flask of whiskey or vodka that I'd hit when no one was around. In a bathroom stall or in the taxi, when I could take it in without notice or reprimand. When I caused too big a scene, I'd start over with a new woman. I'd lay off drinking the way I liked to until they were intrigued with me; and then I'd get comfortable and blow it.

It wasn't a pattern of behavior I designed, but it's one I lived in for too long. When alcohol was involved, I knew it wasn't going to play out well. In spite of plenty of evidence, I continued to test my ability to change course and avoid crashing just in time. Maybe it would play out better if I wore red socks, drank on Tuesday instead of Saturday, ate Spam or gave up meat altogether. If I ran in the morning or meditated at night. None of it made any difference at all.

The physiological reality of an alcoholic is that alcohol consumption breeds craving and tolerance. The disease ensures that the alcoholic's desire for alcohol is by nature, insatiable. The body demands more than one can possibly feed it and the alcoholic will pass out, anchored to the futile effort toward satisfaction. Progression colors the illness most often fatal. The habit of drinking forms, the body behaves alcoholically, the physical need is not sustainable, and the drinker goes insane or dies seeking relief they experienced early on.

Sadly, short of a miracle or successful intervention, a chronic alcoholic has little defense against this playing out. A lifetime of relationships and self-sufficiency will elude the alcoholic before they connect their problems to the bottle. They gradually come to accept that they are tethered to liquor. Cocktails are no longer social, recreational, or optional; they have to drink. They have lost the power of choice when it comes to alcohol.

I'd passed them every day on my way to work and they reminded me of a halfway house Dad lived in for a while when I was young. It was a big house, well kept. Staged in front of the steps was a circle of talkative men, smoking cigarettes and drinking something hot from Styrofoam cups.

It was an atrocious defeat that led me, open minded, to their doorstep at twenty-seven years old. I asked if they had meetings there and they smiled warmly, directing me inside to the basement. I was invited to a second meeting the following week. A woman I'd never met offered to bring me, simply because someone had helped her when she was trying to get sober. I wouldn't be able to pick her out of a line-up today, but I thank God she showed me to my first woman's meeting and encouraged me to get a sponsor.

Mostly I sat quietly and listened to other people speak. I couldn't believe the stories they told; the things that they said out loud! I was intrigued and strangely comfortable. I was grateful they let me sit there quietly. Sometimes a really happy woman would introduce herself, ask my name and say, "Welcome".

I believe I'd be dead today if it weren't for that group of people who welcomed me into their vulnerable journey of recovery from alcoholism. I would have drunk myself to death, or otherwise killed myself had they not been readily available. I could not imagine a life without drinking, but I'd come to see quite clearly that I would have no life at all if I kept going the way I was. I had tried many times for many years. I had changed patterns, gone months without a drop, but always when I took one drink, the inevitable chaos followed soon after. I had to put it down for good.

It's not easy to ask for help, unless you're able to admit defeat. I was prepared to do that with alcohol. I knew that who I was under its command was nothing like who I was meant to be. I had no doubt that I could not safely continue to drink. I put myself in the hands of strangers and took suggestions from a woman who had a year and a half sober at the time. She told me what she did and invited me to do the same. The twelve steps is a process that guides a human being through the cobwebs of a lifetime of habits and a belief system that are killing them. Alcohol is a symptom of a broken personal GPS. Alcohol appears to be a solution at first, pacifying an inability to form healthy relationships with others. Eventually, alcohol creates more problems than it ever solves, but it is still just a symptom of a wayward orientation to reality. The disease of alcoholism lives in the behaviors of the family. The disease is embedded in the people pleasing, the stifling of important conversations, the brushing things under the rug. It is alive in the compliance and concessions and compensations made in the family system and it spans the family tree well beyond the impact of the person using alcohol. I had so much to learn. Thank God I'd been humiliated enough times by my drinking behavior to take direction from those who understood and could help.

When I got to recovery, I learned a lot by listening to people share their personal stories. The community that formed around me is an incredible, courageous community. Many people who find themselves in recovery are very creative and intuitive people who didn't find the support for their sensitivities in everyday life. We have a hard time following rules; not because we are stupid, but because life has taught us that they don't matter. Many of my tribe grew up in alcoholic homes, or dysfunctional families that did not have alcohol or drugs in them. Addiction to alcohol or other things is a family illness. Although there may be only one alcoholic, everyone becomes sick.

The behaviors and survival skills we learned in our childhood home were a precise recipe for dysfunction. Since we memorized how to navigate the family and make habits of what worked, we didn't recognize that we were following instructions to create chaos. I began to suspect there might be a common denominator, and concluded it was the amount of alcohol I was drinking. I was sure that I needed to break up with alcohol to improve my life. What I found was that whether I was drinking or sober, relationships didn't work very well for me until I did a lot of work on myself.

Dating in my twenties had less to do with my sexual orientation and more to do with wanting to belong and fit in. It took too long for me to recognize my pattern of recreating my family relationships that were based on dysfunction. I learned sexuality earlier than I should have. Older girls and boys in the neighborhood got me involved in sexual behaviors before I was ready, before I was eight. I received sexual attention long before I knew my body belonged to me or how to honor myself in sharing it. Through years of detachment and loneliness, then excessive, aggressive drinking, promiscuity became a tool for me. Subconsciously, I was taking power back from early experiences that had left me feeling powerless. Every time I seduced a man or a woman, I was in a position of power. Every time I started to drink to relieve the shame I felt about not behaving well while drunk, it felt like I was in power. I was the initiator, the one taking action, the one doing the seducing. And I continued to do it despite how awful I felt about myself. I was inside the spiral, causing it, yet powerless once again to stop it. Alcohol made it possible. I whined a common cry, "Why does this keep happening to me? What's wrong with me? Am I crazy?"

There are many ways to arrive at surrender in life. For me, to reach my bottom with alcohol was the biggest gift. I needed to find a way of living without substances because my body and behavior betrayed me when I consumed them. I had to learn how to avoid the first drink when feelings surfaced, because I didn't have the luxury of drinking to take the edge off. My alcoholic body would make certain that once I fed it one drink, it would take the keys and be in control going forward.

After I admitted that I couldn't drink and demonstrated a commitment to quitting, I had to do a lot more work on myself, commonly called the Twelve Steps. I had help from a woman who had already done them. I told her I was anxious about the word God when it came up in the different materials we read at meetings. I told her that God wasn't real happy with me and I was afraid that if I had to be on good terms with God to get well, I was fucked.

She told me that God knew everything about me and if I wanted to get sober, God was very pleased with that and would help me. Any problems I had with God I could figure out after I got sober. She said that God would continue to be patient with me. She said I could pray to her Higher Power in the meantime, because it was working for her. That allowed me to take a deep breath. I needed that permission and freedom to meander, so that I could figure out what felt true to me and find my own way.

Around this time, Yuji returned from her trip and performed in a show I was hosting. My relationship with Daya immediately became unnecessarily complicated. By me. I had such deep-rooted codependency issues that seeing

Yuji again triggered a responsibility in me. The out of sight, out of mind that alcoholism accommodated was confronted. I was addicted to the idea of her. She appeared before me in a season of her radiance. The pain we'd been through was too far away to recall. It had only been months, but as she sang a few bars, I was consumed by grief and regret that we hadn't made things work. I had built an identity around the fantasy of loving a singer, and I'd never processed the end of us. Her inner light shone front and center, and in that moment, I could only remember the joy of us.

After the show, Yuji came and spoke with Daya and me, and something kinetic in being near her flipped a switch. In her presence, I couldn't believe that my recollection of us could be true. Yuji told me that I had been mean and cruel, and I believed her. She said she needed time to figure some things out, and asked, "Why would you assume that not hearing from me for a month meant I didn't love you or I wanted to break up?"

Daya kissed my cheek and excused herself, after telling Yuji she had given a wonderful performance. I let her walk away and stood naked in Yuji's question. I had nothing. My experience only made sense until she voiced the question out loud. Suddenly I felt like an asshole, like I was stupid. Ah, sweet, familiar comfort zone.

I fell under the alluring spell of a narrative Yuji weaved, that she never meant to break up with me. Hearing it from her face-to-face and sober, her story sounded completely rational.

What the hell was wrong with me? I wondered.

Prior to seeing Yuji, I was certain that I was in a better relationship with Daya than I'd ever been in my adult life. But seeing Yuji provoked a weakness, a self-doubt that left me ashamed to have been so mistaken. The pattern of relationship missteps was like when a woman shrieking through pregnancy swears she'll never give birth again, because it's fucking insane to be in so much pain. That same woman, after time has passed, will avoid contraception for the fantasy of another baby. She doubts the whisper of reality just long enough to embrace the dream of doing it again.

Not until she has her legs in stirrups with her body ripping and bleeding, does she remember.

Here I had this incredible, inspiring, down-to-earth girl in my life. We didn't argue, fight, or struggle to enjoy each other. We laughed all the time and I wanted to stay. I wanted to trust myself that what I was experiencing with Daya was true, and that I deserved it, but the whispers of my emotional responsibility to Yuji, based on her very different perception of our demise, were strong. I believed I was capable of being mean, as she claimed. Was she in danger from her own demons because of me? That fear drew me closer to her. It was an old familiar burden, to care for someone else before myself.

After that evening, I told Daya that I needed some time to figure out what I was doing, what I was feeling. True to form, her patience was limited when the decision I was struggling with was whether to return to someone with whom I'd shared horrific fights and confusion or stay in a relationship that empowered us both to be the artists and professionals and family members we were together. She was right to not give me the two weeks I requested. She had a life to live.

She came by my apartment one day and presented me with a long list of handwritten, double-spaced reasons why she and I were better together than apart. She sat and held my hand while she read it to me, and I cried.

I knew what was right for me and what I wanted, but my responsibility to the broken relationship with Yuji, and fear that she might hurt herself—which I could never live with— were stronger than what I wanted. I hadn't yet learned to seize healthy moments and step into my power. I hadn't learned to surround myself by people who empowered me, not yet.

When Daya was done, she looked up with tears in her eyes, waiting for my response. I wanted to thank her and tell her I loved her; and yes, I wanted to ignore the interruption of Yuji's return. I felt good about myself with Daya. I respected her and wanted to be like her. I wanted to tell her I chose her because things operate smoothly without tension and doubt causing passive-aggressive meanderings. I wanted to continue to produce theater with her.

I wanted to become the woman she saw in me, because I wasn't that woman yet.

I sat there and knew that she was strong enough to take care of herself. I knew that she didn't need me. I was a luxury. I wanted her too, but Yuji needed me more. Since I didn't know how to articulate all of this at the time, I did my best to at least be honest. So when she said, "What do you think, baby?" I cringe at the words I said next. "I don't know what to do. I'm in love with two women."

Daya shuddered, and tears fell. I bit my tongue to keep from making things worse. She had no appetite for drama like Yuji and I did. Because she knew what she was worth, she gathered her things and stood up to head for the door. I shuffled pathetically behind, telling myself to set her free from the mess that I was. I told myself to let her go but I wanted to keep her close, to ask for her forgiveness. I prayed that she would stay and fight for me, but she turned to me one last time in the open doorway and pushed her index finger forcefully into my chest each time she choked out a word. "Do. *Not*. Let. Her. Hurt. You. *Again*."

And then she was gone.

* * *

I resumed a relationship with Yuji, and shortly afterward things became confusing and complicated again. I realized quickly that I needed to listen to my sponsor and work my program, being cautious about my choices and behaviors in personal relationships. I needed to figure out why I felt responsible for others and stayed in situations that made me feel small and helpless. The work was hard and looking at why I had the habits I did was painful. It wasn't a quick process. Self-discovery is a journey unto itself.

Gratefully, my sponsor grew tired of me whining about my relationship and reminded me that I chose it. She told me she didn't want to hear about it anymore because I kept doing the same thing and expecting different results. That really pissed me off, and also, I heard her. She told me to get a Higher Power and pray for help to change, and to write in my journal before I called her again.

I prayed to my late paternal grandmother. I wasn't ready to talk to God directly yet, so Grandma was the messenger in my prayer life while I worked out the details of my own belief system. I listened to Dr. King and his sermons, I began to read about yoga and Buddhism, and the Bahi faith. Recovery gave me the freedom to pursue spiritual growth on my own terms. I discovered many gifts in faith, hope, love, and letting go of old ideas.

On November 3, 2002 I celebrated 365 days sober, and I cried when I received my one-year-chip at a meeting. I realized that I had been conscious a whole year for the first time since I was twelve years old. For as many times as I had tried to quit, I never managed to stay sober for an entire year. I stood in front of that meeting and wondered if I had the strength to live in all my accumulated sadness without medicine. I saw my life in time-lapse recall as I smiled at Yuji's face in the audience. My mind jumped around rapidly to all of the faces and memories I would have to carry and confront for the rest of my life, without alcohol.

I flashed back to being high on the lawn with Rory and Aretha, at the John Cougar concert. Aretha was a teacher by then at the grade school where I'd attended fifth grade. I'd called my teacher, Ms. Belser, at the number she'd given me several times, only to learn that it was not a working number. I never did go to dinner at her new house. I was disappointed but knew that she was on the planet somewhere and just like we always had, I trusted we would cross paths again. I asked Aretha if she could look into Ms. Belser's whereabouts for me, and I'll never forget the look on her face. As stoned as we were, I sobered immediately when her expression fell.

"Oh, Jen, you don't know?"

The entire world grew silent and cold. All I could see were the words forming cautiously behind my friend's lips. I stared at her, waiting for her to ease the anxiety I felt.

"I overheard some colleagues talking in the teachers break room. They were saying they couldn't believe it was already almost a year since she died of cancer."

I froze and the ground fell out from beneath me. The night swallowed me, and Aretha's face swirled in motion. Had I heard her correctly? Was that why the number didn't work? Maybe it was a different teacher. It couldn't be. Why hadn't she told me she was sick? She would have told me, of all people, right? Cotton mouth nearly choked me, and I reached for a beer.

"Jen, are you okay?"

"I don't think she knew," somebody next to me said. "Look at her face. She didn't know."

"Aretha, are you kidding me right now? Tell me you're kidding," I begged.

"I'm sorry."

"Ms. Belser, or Mrs. Graham?"

"Fifth-grade teacher, right? She was at Lincoln Elementary. District 88. Yeah, Jen. I'm so sorry."

As I took my year chip, I felt the choke hold of Ms. Belser's absence from Earth. I had nothing I could consume to feel differently, nothing to numb it or push the sadness deep down the way I always had before. I hope I can do this for the rest of my life, but as they say, I have to focus on one day at a time.

I thought of my late angel teacher and the promise she made me make to her in her car years earlier. With a sense of responsibility and determination, I thanked her in my heart before leaning into the microphone.

"Thank you, family. I'm Jen and I'm an alcoholic. And I'm going to keep coming back."

It is suggested that you not be in a romantic relationship in your first year of recovery, so that you can focus on the work you need to do to change your life. I didn't listen, because I was already in the throes of Yuji and Daya drama when I arrived. I was with Yuji when I celebrated one year sober, and she eventually found Al-anon, which is a twelve-step program for family members of the alcoholic. After she and I had both worked the twelve steps with a sponsor, we learned a lot about ourselves. Ultimately, we were able to recognize that although we loved each other, we were never compatible. She and I dissolved our relationship over coffee, with tears in our eyes, and wished each other happiness.

That was the first of many difficult but liberating, grown-up things I'd be called to do in sobriety. Recovery called me to align my behavior with my personal truth, which required vulnerability. It offered a set of spiritual principles to live by, as well as a built-in, worldwide community for support and camaraderie. Together, having surrendered and followed suggestions, the program's guidance and fellowship have helped me navigate a path to gaining and maintaining physical sobriety. To truly begin the alignment, I needed to be free of alcohol and free of that relationship. I had to be willing to stop relying exclusively on myself and ask for help. I needed to address the way I valued myself, I had to be willing to question what I believed as true. That much I knew. I hoped to discover the woman I was capable of being and become her—energized by the original source of comfort I knew as a little girl. I wanted to reconcile my relationship with the power that allowed me to be curious and playful, safe and free. I wanted to become child-like again, spinning and laughing, high on nothing more than fresh air, curiosity, and caffeine.

Made in the USA
Lexington, KY
03 June 2019